WILD IRISH CHRISTMAS

A Mystic Cove and Isle of Destiny festive novella

TRICIA O'MALLEY

Lovewrite Publishing

"Some day you will be old enough to start reading fairy tales again." – C.S. Lewis

Chapter One

A LOUD BANG shot Lily Walden from her bed, her hand reaching for the cricket bat she'd leaned against the wall. For a moment, confusion raced through her as she struggled to pull her brain from the delicious dream she'd been having to determine where, exactly, she was.

Right, then. She was in the small one-bedroom cottage she'd just moved to in the hills outside Grace's Cove. She was safe, Lily reminded herself, even as her heart raced in her chest.

When the bang sounded again, she realized it was a shutter that had come loose in the wind, and flipped on a light to attend to the matter. Catching a glimpse in the mirror, Lily sighed. Even to herself she looked like a shivering, frightened mouse.

It was the name he'd always called her. First as a pet name, and then in a derogatory way. His little mouse. Once she'd thought it sweet, before it had become a taunt. Her eyes, huge in her small face, were a deep boring brown, and her hair was one of those right-in-the-middle browns.

Not a rich mahogany, nor was it shot through with golden highlights. With delicate features, a slight build, and a propensity to get lost in her dreams, Lily lived up to the name her mother had given her. If she were the lily-pad part, that is.

More like a doormat, Lily berated herself as she opened the window to let in a few spatterings of ice-cold rain before pulling the shutter closed and firmly shoving the hook in place.

Lily's mother had always been prone to flights of fancy. When she'd found out she was pregnant with a girl, she'd immediately picked the name Lily, fancying her daughter to be as beautiful as a trip to Thoreau's Walden Pond. Never once had her mum led her to think differently, but Lily couldn't help but wonder if she was disappointed with her daughter, a quiet schoolteacher who'd let a man take over her world.

"Not anymore," Lily said fiercely to nobody in particular. She was making her own decisions now.

It had been the first time he'd hit her. Lily had known, without a doubt, as she lay on the floor clutching her cheek, that it also wouldn't be the last – unless she worked up the courage to stand up for herself, that is. It wasn't until she'd snuck away in the middle of the night, clear to the other side of Ireland, that she'd finally started to find the thread of who she was once again. She'd lost it, for years, tangled up in Bruce's demands, and he'd groomed her to keep her opinions to herself and to be at his beck and call. Even when she was perfect, Lily had still been reprimanded, and silent fury had begun to burn deep in her soul.

A part of her wished it hadn't taken Bruce's fists to finally give her the courage to leave, but nevertheless, she was proud of the steps she'd taken. Lily was determined to start living life on her terms, and finding this little cottage snuggled in the hills outside the darling town of Grace's Cove had seemed like just the sign she'd needed. She'd never been to this town before, in fact had hardly known it existed. Yet, when she'd made the decision to leave, it had been like a neon sign blinking in her brain – THIS WAY.

Lily had followed that instinct, and once she'd arrived, all of the pieces seemed to be falling neatly in place for her. She was to start her new job as a preschool teacher after the Christmas holiday. She'd been lucky there, to find a job this close to Christmas, but it sounded like the last teacher had found love in England and wouldn't be returning.

Grateful for work, Lily had accepted under one condition – that her students would call her Ms. Lewis. When the head of the school, a lovely woman named Mary, had shot her a questioning look, Lily just explained she'd had a bad break-up. Nodding once, Mary had accepted the explanation, patted her on the back, and welcomed her to the school.

With that, Lily got to start her brand-new life.

She scrambled back to the pretty wrought-iron bed, piled high with pillows and a handmade quilt. The rain pounded harder outside, and Lily snuggled in, feeling… calm for the first time in ages. She wondered if she was brave enough to take the next step she craved.

What if she embraced her dreams?

Lily paused when a warm feeling spread through her,

almost like her heart was dancing. It was a secret dream, buried so long, that she had stopped pulling it out to look at it. But here it was, and maybe now was the time to finally embrace it.

Lily wanted to write fairy tales.

It was silly, maybe, and even escapist at times, but she quite often lost herself in very rich, almost lifelike daydreams. Those dreams would then continue at night, and there it was like she was living as a different person. A fierce woman who owned her space in the world, Lily danced through magickal realms and made men fall at her feet. There had been one man, over the past two years, that had particularly caught her fancy. A prince of the fae, mercurial and magick, and he'd been slipping into her dreams almost every night now. Her hands itched to sketch him.

Instead, she closed her eyes and brought his face to mind, smiling to herself when a warm trickle of excitement slipped through her. It wasn't like seeing an old friend – it was like discovering a new lover.

At that thought, Lily giggled and slapped a hand over her mouth. To even think of taking a lover again was something that was so absurd, she wasn't even sure why the thought had entered her mind. Bruce hadn't broken her, but he'd done his damnedest. Lily didn't think she'd be able to allow herself to be that vulnerable to anyone anytime soon.

But she could dream, couldn't she?

Callum. His name came unbidden to her lips. Silver-haired, dark eyed, and a tinge of purple glowing around him. Lily wondered if purple was the color of royalty in the fae world or if it was simply his aura. Not that she could see auras, but in her dreams that didn't seem to matter. Either way, magick all but sparkled around him, and he moved with a fluidity and grace that belied his large, muscular build.

Humming a song that she'd only heard in her dreams, Lily slipped into sleep, secure in the beginnings of her new life.

Chapter Two

CALLUM WHIPPED his head up as the song came to him across the water. For months now…nay, even years, the tune had haunted him. He'd sought it out time and time again, only to lose the song in his search for her. It was as though the music danced on the wind, twirling and teasing him, forever leaving him aching for the woman who called to him.

His one true love.

He'd known the instant he'd heard the first note of the first song – a song he only sang in his dreams – that his love called to him. Like a siren from the shore, she beckoned him closer, singing to him his love song, the one only his fated mate could know.

Nobody had told him it would be this hard.

As prince of the Danula fae, he'd known challenges in his life. His kingdom had been threatened for years. Callum had plunged his way fearlessly into battle for ages, always certain of the outcome. Yet now, as the last of the notes lingered on the horizon, his stomach twisted. Defeat wasn't something he could accept. Why couldn't he find her?

"What's wrong with you?" Nolan, his best friend and a fae almost as powerful as Callum, came to stand next to him on the rocky shoreline. A squall had kicked up, mirroring Callum's mood, spitting shards of ice at them. Neither man moved as they studied the churning ocean.

"It matters little."

"It does at that. Look at the water fae. They're positively mad with this weather you've churned up. You can see them gnashing their teeth as they ride the waves."

"They do delight in a little turmoil, don't they?" Callum laughed as one fae rode a wave so high in the air that he flipped several times before plopping back into the churning mess of dark water below him. A tendril of blue followed his plummet back into the inky depths. If a human looked at the water, they would claim it was bioluminescence.

It was better that way.

Callum had long been a holdout in the belief that the fae and the human world should not blend. Certain instances required it, like the time when the Four Treasures had to be recovered, so allowances were made. However, it was his belief that separate was the better – and the smarter – way of co-existing with humans. It was an unpopular belief with many of the fae, who were consistently enchanted with humans and viewed them as great entertainment. For Callum, the less interaction with the human race was the safest choice – for both sides.

"Is it her?" Nolan asked.

"Aye, she calls to me again. It's getting stronger now. I don't understand why I can't find her."

"Maybe it wasn't the right time?"

"Then why call to me all these months? It makes no sense." Callum swore and turned, striding up the sodden beach to where a creviced entrance in a rock wall held a portal to their world. "The books say that the call comes when lovers are ready to meet."

"Maybe you weren't ready to meet her?" Nolan asked, stopping when Callum did.

"What did you say to me?" Callum turned and shot Nolan a look through slanted eyes.

Undeterred, Nolan gave Callum a grin. "Well, you've been pretty busy with overseeing a few strategic battles. I didn't exactly hear you singing to her over the waters, now, did I?"

"I sang to her," Callum protested.

"When?"

"I…well, in my dreams."

"You dreamwalked to her? What does she look like?" Nolan crossed his arms and leaned against the rock wall. Both fae ignored the rain that now pelted down in sheets.

"I…I didn't speak with her."

"So you stalked her. In your dreams. But didn't try to find her in real life?"

"I told you, I've tried to find her in real life. I've nothing to go on."

"Let's have a look at your dreams then. Come, we'll have a pint and discuss." With the confidence of a best friend, and one of the few allowed to do so, Nolan cut in front of the prince and squeezed through the crevice.

With one last lingering glance out to the churning waters, Callum slipped through behind Nolan and into his study. It was handy, the magick he had, for when he entered a fae portal, he could go directly to his home instead of being deposited into a city and having to move about from there. Not all fae were afforded such luxuries, but it was a magick that was quite pleasing to Callum.

"Whiskey?"

"Aye, stronger than a pint; I need it," Callum agreed, and dropped into a leather chair tucked in front of a fire. His eyes sought the flames, looking for any messages in the fire, but none came for him that way. The fire fae kept their secrets to themselves on this stormy night.

"Slainté," Nolan said, and they clinked their glasses together before Nolan plopped into the chair across from Callum. "Tell me about the lass."

"She's…" Callum angled his head and studied the fire as he thought about what he'd seen in his dreams. "Ethereal, almost. Fine-boned, delicate, and eyes that would make a man drop to his knees were they ever to beg of him. But…"

"But?"

"Her power is dull. From the few times I've been able to seek her out, it's as though her light has been shaded. It's not out, but considerably dimmed. I don't know who has done this to her."

"You think she has been spelled?"

"Perhaps, though I couldn't glean by whom. I didn't discern any tendrils of magick around her."

"Where was she? What did the surroundings look like? Perhaps we could track her in a different manner."

"You've raised a good point, you have," Callum said. He tipped his whiskey at Nolan before sipping it again, letting the heat slide over his tongue as he closed his eyes and thought back to when he'd last dreamed of her.

She'd looked…pained, he supposed was the best word for it. Tense, shoulders hunched, all but hiding in a corner as she went through her day. Her dress had mirrored her mood, a simple, gray, shapeless sort of thing, and she'd wound an equally boring scarf around her neck to ward off the cold. But the eyes…the fire still burned bright there. He wondered what she would look like draped in the silks he could provide her with. A radiant purple would warm her skin tone and caress her delicate shape.

His hand tightened on the glass at the thought, as though he could touch her, and Callum opened his eyes once again. "The thing is, I've nothing yet that shows me where she is. Every time I've dreamed of her, she's been inside, either in a house or at what looks to be a school. No indication of where."

"A fae school?"

"Well, of course…" Callum trailed off. "Are you telling me you think she's not fae?"

Thunder plummeted the walls of the castle, and Nolan raised a hand as though to soothe Callum. "I'm merely saying it would be easy to tell if the school was fae. Homes can be trickier to ascertain. But a school? How old were the children?"

"Young…" Callum bit out.

"Aye, you know how they are at that age. Completely out of control of their powers. Was there anything floating through the air? Any magicks lingering? Spilled pixie dust? Think about it."

"There wasn't." Callum's breath hitched.

"And how many schools do we have here that look like hers?"

"None," Callum whispered.

"So is there a chance she's human?"

"How can that be? I'm a prince! Aren't we meant to be fated with magickal beings?"

"I don't know if that is the rule or just what is common among royals. I don't believe it's frowned upon. Look at Na Cosantoir – the Protectors. Your own bloodline. Your brethren. They've all matched with humans to much success. I've never seen them happier. Why would it be such a stretch for you to believe that a human is your mate?"

"Because…because…it's just. No. It can't be. I'm certain that's not the situation."

"Aye, I understand it could shake you up a wee bit. Maybe sit with the thought for a while? Can you try having a dreamwalk with her tonight? This time pay particular attention to her surroundings. Maybe you'll be getting some clues and we can go on a bit of a hunt."

"You want to find her with me?"

"Aye, and why not? I've nothing better to do when you've brought the weather down with your mood."

"I did no such thing."

"Didn't you?" Nolan stood and patted Callum's shoulder before exiting the study in search of a warm and willing woman, of that Callum was sure.

Was it possible she was human? The thought had never

once crossed his mind, and now it hovered there laughing at him and all the clues he'd missed along the way. Of course he'd never seen her do magick. In fact, he'd never seen any sort of magick in her aura. He'd been so entranced with her features and her shy smile that not once had he even looked for her magickal signature.

Cursing, he finished his whiskey and left the study to wind his way down a corridor lit with lanterns that danced patterns across the walls. Reaching a curved wood door, he pressed his hand to the door, unlocking it with his magick, and entered his sacred magicks space.

The room, a complete circle with no windows, had a glistening white marble floor clear of adornment. Shelves lined the wall carrying various ingredients that he could use in his magickal work as needed. But Callum needed no spell to reach his mate – all he had to do was call to her. Laying himself down in the middle of the circular floor, Callum closed his eyes and began to sing.

"Larraim ort mo ghrá…"

Chapter Three

LILY HAD TAKEN to walking the hills since she'd moved to Grace's Cove.

She had a good pair of waterproof boots and an over-sized rain jacket that fit over a soft wool sweater. The brisk wind didn't bother her, nor did the occasional pelting rain. If anything, the drops of rain that stung her face reminded her that she hadn't gone entirely numb to the world. The hills had become a refuge of sorts, the earth all but singing to her as she rambled, the tension she'd carried for years seeming to slip from her shoulders along with the rain and melt into the ground at her feet. It had only been a matter of weeks since she'd arrived, but already she'd begun to feel at home.

She'd started writing her first actual book last night. Different than the dreams she'd copied down for years now, this was her own story of her own creation.

Lily hugged her arms around herself and laughed, turning her face up to the sky and letting the rain slick down her cheeks. A fire burned inside her, one she'd lit herself, and she was tentatively happy with herself for the first time that she could remember.

Sure, there had been some stumbles to get the words down on the page. But after she'd finally given over to what she really wanted to write – instead of the story she had dutifully outlined ages ago – the words had simply flowed.

It was about the Fae Prince. Naturally.

Writing about him had made her pen fly across the pages as though she'd done this every day of her life. And yes, she was writing with a pen. Lily laughed at herself once again, shaking her head a little against the romantic image presented in her mind of her head bent over the little leather notebook while the light from the fire danced with the shadows on the wall. The small Christmas tree she'd bought and decorated with a strand of twinkle lights had beamed at her from its corner by the fire. It had been lonely, decorating the tree by herself, but the loneliness slipped away as her story came to life before her. She'd have to go back and type every last word of it out, she *knew* that, and yet something was drawing her to write this story by hand.

Her very first fairy tale.

So what if her writing wasn't great? Before she'd started, Lily had written out a list of ground rules for her writing. The most important one? Write without self-judgment. She was giving herself full permission to let the story flow, and later on she would deal with any cringe-worthy moments. Once she'd taken any restrictions off, the words had come to her and she'd spent a large part of the night huddled in the chair by the fire lost in her own thoughts.

It was her favorite place to be, after all.

Lily drew up short as she neared a cliff wall, her inner alarm telling her to stop daydreaming and pay attention to her footing. Judging from the sounds of the waves far below, it would be a mighty fall if she tripped and went over the edge. Her walks hadn't taken her this way yet, and now she wondered why she didn't come here daily.

The spot, quite simply, was magnificent.

Stretched before her was a cove hugged by cliff walls that jutted proudly into the sky as though to challenge any who dared enter it. The cliffs very nearly touched, and the passage into the cove from farther out in the water looked difficult to navigate for even the most seasoned of sailors. A little trail switchbacked down the cliff wall, and a part of Lily really wanted to race down to the beach and dream away her afternoon surrounded by such staggering beauty. Instead, she glanced down to the wet ground and the narrow path, and stepped back.

"Best not to," Lily said to herself, "you'll likely slip and bounce all the way to the bottom, and land in a broken heap. And wouldn't that just destroy the beauty of this spot? No, I think it's best not to explore."

Though her confidence was growing each day, Lily still struggled with her timid nature. Baby steps, she promised herself, and started to turn from the cove.

"Larraim ort mo ghrá…"

A whisper against her skin, a song on the wind, a shiver in her heart… Lily gasped and turned back to the cove as a brilliant light shone from the depths. It shimmered in the water as Callum sang to her on the wind, and tears mingled with the rain on Lily's cheeks.

Had she finally gone mad?

If so, maybe this was the world she deserved to live in. Lily slapped a hand over her mouth to stop the breathless giggle that bordered on hysteria from bubbling out. Hearing voices on the wind, dreaming of handsome magickal princes, and seeing the ocean glow from within were all the things of her fantasies. Was she still living back with Bruce? Maybe Lily had finally checked completely out and now twirled away from danger into the inner recesses of her mind.

"Ground yourself, Lily," she ordered.

She opened her eyes to find the shimmering light had gone from the ocean below. Turning, she tilted her head to the sky, feeling the coldness of the rain against her skin. She crouched and dug her fingers into the dirt, and pulled a blade of grass to her nose. It smelled of musty wet dirt, but the particularly sharp scent of grass made her believe this was real. No imagination was *that* good…was it? She could see, smell, and likely even taste her surroundings. But if she hadn't gone crazy…then what was really happening?

Lily jumped as thunder rattled the sky, and she realized, dreaming or not, she'd better get moving to her car or she was about to be caught in a very nasty storm. Leaving the cove behind, along with her questions, Lily raced across the hills and slammed the door of her little car before a nasty sheet of rain hit the window. Despite herself, a nervous giggle escaped her. Even if she was going mental, this wasn't a particularly bad place to be.

Shaking off the thoughts, Lily pulled the car into gear and slowly made her way along the tiny road that hugged the cliffs back into town. As she neared, she could see the brightly lit pub that she'd passed several times but had never gone inside. Maybe it would be nice to stop for a bite instead of having to prepare her dinner alone.

On a whim, she pulled the car into a spot and rushed inside in a flurry of wind and rain, the door banging loudly behind her. A few heads turned and nodded at her, but apparently people must be used to women tumbling into the pub during a storm, as nobody acted all that bothered by her disheveled entrance.

A slight woman with a sharp, no-nonsense look in her eye manned the long expanse of bar crafted from a richly colored wood. Glass shelves lined a mirrored wall behind the bar, and the pub area opened out into a room full of booths and tables, which Lily imagined could be cleared for a dance or two. Christmas garlands were twined around the booths, and twinkle lights were strung across the ceiling in long arcs. The space was charming, and homey, and made Lily's heart twinge as she thought about spending Christmas alone this year. Unsure if she was bold enough to sit at the bar, Lily looked around for an empty table. Unsurprisingly, the room was full. The Irish did like going to the pub during inclement weather.

"There's a spot down here." The woman behind the bar nodded to an area Lily couldn't quite see from the door.

Smiling her thanks, Lily took off her coat and hung it with the others dripping next to the door. Nodding awkwardly at a few people who smiled at her, she rushed across the room and out of sight of the main crowd. When the sound of the door slamming again came behind her, Lily breathed out a sigh of relief. Someone else for the crowd to stare at had arrived. She looked around but did not see a spot to sit, and shot a questioning glance at the woman behind the bar.

"Did you say there was a spot?"

"Aye love, we've got a spot. Come join us."

Lily turned to see a beanpole of man with a shock of red hair threaded with gray tucked cozily next to a curvy blonde in a booth. The seat across the table was empty. Both of them looked to be in their late forties or early fifties, and had welcoming smiles on their faces.

"Oh, if you're sure? I don't want to interrupt. I just thought I'd get a quick bite on my way home from the cove."

"Oh, you've been visiting the cove then? In this weather? Aren't you a bold one?" The woman nodded at the table, and Lily slid into the booth, smiling at them both.

"I don't reckon that I've ever been called bold before, I have to say," Lily confided, heat tinging her cheeks.

"Is that right? I'm surprised at that. My name is Bianca, and this handsome lad is the love of me life, Seamus."

"Nice to meet you. My name is Lily."

Introductions done, Lily paused as a waitress stopped at the table. "The special tonight is a roasted tomato soup with a cheese toastie on the side."

"Perfect comfort food. I'll take an order of that."

"To drink?"

"Oh, just a tea, please. I'm driving."

The waitress nodded and breezed away without writing her order down and stuck her head through a door to bark orders at someone in the back. Lily turned as a lilting Irish tune came from a booth in front and smiled when a little toddler ran into the middle of the room and began to bounce his bum to the music.

"That one's going to drive her crazy." Bianca nodded to the baby. "But it certainly won't be a boring life."

"No, it won't," Seamus agreed, and stretched back in his seat, dropping his arm casually around Bianca's shoulders. His eyes narrowed at Lily for a moment, and tension crept up her neck at his assessment. Living a life with someone like Bruce had taught her to read other people's emotions well. There was something…off about Seamus.

"Have I something on my face?" Lily challenged him, and a grin spread over his face once again.

"No, I'm sorry for staring at you. You're right lovely, is all. If I wasn't besotted with my girl here, I'd be asking you for a date."

Lily's eyes flew to Bianca's to see if the woman was upset.

"He's the right of it, at that. I'd burn his eyes out with a poker if I knew he really fancied you, but my man is a loyal one. Plus, you are lovely. Not many people can come in from a storm without looking like a drowned rat. You look as though the weather lit you up."

"I…well, thank you." Lily laughed softly, "That's kind of you both. I don't feel like a drowned rat at all. In fact, I feel a bit exhilarated."

"The cove got to you, didn't it? It grabs a hold of one's soul," Bianca nodded at her.

"It really does, doesn't it? I…well, I'm positive I was going mad out there. Perhaps it was just exposure to the elements." Lily shrugged off what she was going to say with a little laugh as her food was delivered to the table along with a steaming pot of tea in a cheerful blue pot covered in daisies. She took a spoonful of soup into her mouth to stop herself from babbling.

"The cove has quite a history of working its magick on people," Bianca said. "Perhaps you're one of them who feels it there."

"I…" Lily took a bite of her toastie and shrugged, keeping her answer noncommittal, though her eyes darted between the two strangers across from her.

"Are you traveling through, Lily? Having a holiday?" Seamus asked, taking a sip of his Guinness as he studied her with eyes she was starting to feel saw too much.

"No, um, actually I've recently moved here. I'll start my new job after the holiday break."

"Is that right? Welcome to Grace's Cove." Bianca beamed at her before turning to shout to the woman behind the bar, "Cait, Lily is new to town. Be sure to introduce her around when she comes in."

"Oh, well, no need to…" Lily trailed off as Cait materialized in front their table.

"My name is Cait and this is my pub. You're welcome here…"

"Lily," Lily finished for her, and shook her hand. Cait held a beat longer and studied her before dropping it. Like with Seamus, Lily got an odd feeling, as though she was being dissected. "Thank you, it's a lovely spot."

"It's where you'll go for all the village news. First

meal's on me as a welcome gift. Can I top anyone else off?" Cait nodded as Seamus held up his almost empty pint and breezed away. A woman in motion who stayed in motion, Lily thought.

"That was nice of her."

"Cait's a good one. Looks after this town and knows everything you'll need to be knowing," Seamus said.

"I don't think I'll need to know too much," Lily said. "I mainly keep to myself."

"Why is that?" Bianca asked.

"Um, I…" Lily blushed and admonished herself for not being more forward. Why was it she kept to herself so much? In the past, it had been because Bruce was the life of the party and she was always in the background to tend to his needs. "Honestly? I don't rightly know. I think it's time to change that."

"Well, then, we'll be glad to see you around here." Bianca beamed at her. "I have to imagine it's right difficult to be up and moving to a new place on your own for Christmas."

"I suppose, it is," Lily allowed, taking another spoonful of soup. "I didn't have much choice in the timing of my move, but I'll make the most of it. That's what Christmas is for, right? Believing in new beginnings?"

"It is at that," Bianca studied her.

Lily couldn't help but think of her past Christmases. Bruce had loved to entertain and he'd always thrown a lavish Christmas party where he was the center of attention and she scurried around attending to everyone's needs. More often than not, she'd spent most of the time in the kitchen while Bruce held court in the living room. After a time, she'd told herself she didn't mind so much – being in the kitchen had left her alone with her daydreams.

"Do you both live here as well?" Lily asked.

"Here and there. We travel a lot, but come back to Grace's Cove frequently. It's a landing spot for our kids as well, now that they are off at uni." Bianca sighed and shook her head.

"It's a fantastic spot to land. Sort of just welcomes you right in, doesn't it? At least, it felt that way to me," Lily said.

"It definitely has a pull for particular people," Seamus said. "Tell me, Lily…it sounded like you were going to say something else about the cove. Did you feel something out there?"

"Feel something? Oh, well, just that it's lovely?" Lily blinked at him and did her best to transmit sincerity.

"Oh, she's got that look down cold, doesn't she?" Bianca laughed and nudged Seamus. "Almost had you believing her with those big doe eyes of hers."

"Pardon me?" Lily asked.

"The cove. It's magick. Surely you've heard the stories?" Bianca grinned at her as Lily's world tilted.

"Magick?"

"Aye, that's what I said, didn't I? It's time you learned a little bit about where you landed."

"Oh…maybe I do need a drink after all," Lily said faintly, holding her hand to her pounding chest.

"Best to have one. We'll find you a way home."

Chapter Four

"SURELY YOU CAN'T MEAN actual magick," Lily scoffed, and then took a big gulp of the cider that Bianca had gone and retrieved from the bar. She let the cool, crisp taste of the cider tamp down the heat that twisted in her stomach at their words. Ever cautious, Lily couldn't be certain they weren't trying to have a laugh at her expense.

"It sounds ridiculous, I know. But you can't be Irish without having heard of the fae, right?" Bianca asked.

"Of course." Lily nodded. Or dreamed of them, she silently added.

"So, we Irish have a long history rich in Celtic mythology and..." Bianca shot Seamus a glare when he poked her in the ribs and laughed. "Sure, and you aren't shutting me up, are you then?"

"This isn't one of your university tours. Can't you tell the girl is flummoxed? She can't decide if we're having her on or not. And I'm sensing trust is a big thing for her. So skip the lectures and tell her something that makes her trust us."

"Lectures? I was *not* lecturing. I was merely letting her know that the Irish have a rich history – both oral and written – about magick, and that only a fool would think it's only fiction."

"There are a lot of fools out there," Seamus said.

"Aye, there are. And I'm thinking you could be one of them for interrupting me in such a rude manner. To think, I've given up the best years of my life for a man who won't even let me speak."

"It's an honor, it has been, to be at your side, my beautiful angel. I was merely pointing out that this lovely creature here is looking a tad overwhelmed, and before she bolts on us thinking we're a pair of nutters, it might be good to spend some time addressing her fears."

"Is that true? You're going to leave on us?" Bianca turned and demanded of Lily.

"I…" Lily's mouth dropped open, but there was something about Bianca that demanded honesty. "I, well, yes, I was going to try and make a discreet run for it, as you are making me nervous."

"See?" Seamus said, and then covered a laugh with a cough as Bianca glared at him.

"Lily…" Bianca leaned over and patted her arm.

Normally, Lily would have flinched at someone touching her, but there was something oddly comforting about these two even if they were speaking of wild and fantastical things. "Yes?" she said.

"We are in a unique position here, with you. Is it possible that you can suspend disbelief for a bit and hear us out? Maybe consider us mentors of a sort?"

"Mentors?" Seamus laughed and then buried his nose in his Guinness at another look from Bianca.

"Um, I'm not sure what that means exactly. In connection with the cove, that is. I mean, I know what a mentor is," Lily said.

"Great. How about this – you hear us out, and after you can decide if we're mental or not. Honestly, it's probably not the worst thing we've been called over the years." Bianca poked Seamus. "Mainly due to him, of course. I'm the normal one."

"Rightly so, my love. It wouldn't do to walk too far on the path of normalcy. Can you imagine? What a staid and boring life that would be." Seamus shuddered dramatically and teased a smile from Lily.

"Right, okay then. I'm not sure what to make of the both of you, but I don't get the intention you mean to be harming me. So, yes, I'll listen. Plus, if I'm honest, my curiosity is piqued."

"See? I knew she'd have the gumption to stay." Bianca nodded at Lily with approval.

"I can't decide if I'm the one slowly losing my sanity, so we can just add this interaction to the list until I figure it out." Lily laughed when both Bianca and Seamus gasped and held their hands to their hearts, pretending to be mortally wounded.

"She thinks we're figments of her imagination. I can't tell you how pleased that makes me," Bianca declared. "I've always wanted to be a magickal creature."

"You're magick to me, my love. You are the sparkly dust that dreams are built upon." Seamus beamed at Bianca.

"See why I keep him around?" Bianca asked Lily before planting a smacking kiss on Seamus's cheek.

"I don't blame you," Lily laughed.

"Well, then, since I'm being told I lecture and am being too long-winded, I'll just do a quick crash course on Grace's Cove for you. The cove, as we told you, is magick."

"Right," Lily said, and took another sip of her cider.

"The magick comes from the cove being the famous pirate queen Grace O'Malley's final resting place. Strong blood magick. She chose that spot as hers, and with a blood sacrifice, she enchanted it. Her granddaughter was born on the beach that very day, as Grace gave her soul to the ether, and the bloodline was blessed with her gifts."

"That's…intense," Lily decided. It was intense, but also glorious and magickal, and oh…she could just picture the scene playing out on the shore of the cove deep below the jagged cliffs.

"With the enchantment, the cove has a soul of its own. Because of this, it has a few particular traits that are known to all who live here. Well, the main one is known to all who live here."

"Which is?" Lily asked.

"For those who don't believe in magick, they think there is a strong and dangerous rip current and undertow that can take lives quickly. For those who do believe in magick, the understanding is that you can't enter the beach without an offering."

"An offering? Like killing off your firstborn?" Lily gasped.

"Oh my! You do have an imagination." Bianca laughed

and turned to Seamus, "Could you imagine that? The cove would be horrified."

"I'm sorry, what do you mean by offering then?"

"Something meaningful to you. A necklace. Some beautiful rocks you gathered. That kind of thing. Intention matters more than what the actual offering is. You see, there are treasures buried in the waters of the cove. She protects them. If those who enter mean harm, she'll get rid of them."

"So, you go down to the beach, give your gift and then what?"

"You tell the cove you mean no harm. She'll know if you are telling the truth or not."

"That sounds a bit nerve-rattling, no? I'm a nervous sort. What if she misreads my intentions?" Lily demanded.

"Then I wouldn't go to the cove until you can be certain she'll read you true," Seamus said.

"Is that why…" Lily trailed off and shook her head.

"Why what?" Bianca asked.

"Never mind. You said there was other magick there? What is it?"

"Another magick known to the more magickly-touched folk of this fine village is that the cove will glow from within in the presence of true love."

"I'm sorry…what?" Lily gasped and held her hand to her mouth.

"You saw the light, didn't you?" Seamus shot Lily a knowing look.

"I…" Lily gulped her cider.

"She saw it. That was what she was going to ask

earlier. But you didn't tell us you were with anyone."
Bianca tilted her head in question at Lily.

"Wait…you're just going to accept that I saw a myste-
rious light shining from the depths of the ocean?" Lily's
gaze bounced between the two of the them, trying to read
their emotions.

"Of course. We just told you that it happens, didn't
we?" Bianca said.

"But…I was alone. So that's just silly." Lily leaned
back in disgust. Even when she did buy into the fairy tale,
she still didn't get the Prince. Instead, it was Silly Lily, as
the kids used to call her, fantasizing too much and never
quite fitting in.

"Were you alone?" Seamus asked.

"Of course, I told you I was, didn't I? Do you see
anyone with me?" Lily looked around in exaggeration. "I
came straight from the cove."

"I don't think I've heard any instances where the light
shines for someone without it being about love," Bianca
mused. "Maybe the cove is trying to send you a message."

"What kind of message? That my one true love is
myself?" Lily demanded, surprised to feel anger lancing
through her.

"Well, it's a good thing to love yourself, that it is,"
Bianca said, and reached across the table once more to
squeeze Lily's hand. "Are you doing all right then?"

"I'm not, no." Lily realized that the anger was sliding
dangerously close to tears. "I just…this is so stupid, but I just
wanted to be part of a fairy tale for an instant. Even if you
guys were putting me on. I guess I just needed to believe."

"You *can* believe. We're not putting you on. The both of us? We've been through a lot. Some of which you would never believe." Bianca kept Lily's hand in hers. "We aren't saying that the cove was misfiring or something. We're trying to figure out its message for you. It always has a message, and usually it is about the greatest power of all realms – love."

"And nobody loves me." Lily drooped.

"I don't think that's true. Lily, can you tell me anything unusual that happened to you before you saw the cove shine? Anything you saw or something you were thinking about?" Seamus asked.

"Larraim ort mo ghrá…" Lily said automatically, and paused when Seamus's eyes widened.

"What's that look for, Seamus? You know something. Spill," Bianca demanded.

"Where did you hear that?" Seamus asked, ignoring Bianca, which would not go in his favor, Lily thought, as Bianca's eyes narrowed.

"In my dreams," Lily whispered. "On the wind. At the cove…over the water."

"It's Irish. 'I call for you, my love,'" Bianca deciphered. "But what does this mean? Seamus, you'd better speak."

"She's a fated mate," Seamus whispered.

"Excuse me?" Lily said. "I'm a what?"

"You're a fated mate. A mate to one of me own kind. Likely a very powerful one if you are hearing his song on the wind."

A wave of emotions slammed through Lily so suddenly

that she had to grip the table, and little spots danced in front of her eyes.

"Easy, love. Just breathe," Bianca said, squeezing her hand.

"You can't be serious. And what do you mean, one of your kind?"

"Oh, Seamus? He's fae. Most can't see it, though, so he passes easily as human." Bianca laughed as Lily's eyes went wide in her face. "It's a lot to take in, I know. Took me a fair bit to understand. But I've always loved Celtic mythology, and had hoped some of the grand legends were true. Luckily for me, I found my magick and my love all wrapped in one."

"I…I…"

"Here, drink." Bianca handed Lily her glass, and she drained it in one long slug. "If you're hearing him on the wind…this can't be the first time he's tried to contact you, is it?"

"No," Lily whispered. Her heart felt like it wanted to leap out of her chest and run all the way back to the cove to see if what they were saying was true.

"How does he contact you?" Seamus pressed.

"My dreams." Lily held her hand to her lips. "He comes to me in my dreams and sings me a song. I find myself singing it as I walk the hills these days."

"You're calling to him. A fated mate sings a love song only the other will know. I suspect he's quite desperate to find you if you've been singing to him for a while now. Likely the lad is going a bit crazy." Seamus laughed.

"You say that I'm driving a magickal fae man mad

with lust for wanting me?" Lily started laughing until tears dripped down her face and Bianca handed her a napkin.

"Here, love, dry the waterworks before you have the whole pub coming over to see what's so funny."

"I just…it's beyond the realm of anything I can understand. Mousy Lily driving a fae prince crazy."

"Prince?" Seamus sat up.

"A prince, is he? Good on you then." Bianca nodded approvingly.

"Callum is his name," Lily supplied shyly, and then hairs on the back of her neck stood up when the color drained from Seamus's face.

"What's that look for, Seamus?" Bianca's head moved between the two of them like she was watching a ping-pong match.

"Prince Callum. Prince of the Danula, next in line to the throne," Seamus whispered, and then bowed his head respectfully to Lily.

"Why are you bowing to me?" Lily demanded.

"Congratulations, my soon-to-be queen. You are getting your fairy tale after all."

Chapter Five

CALLUM'S EYES FLEW OPEN.

She'd heard him. Of that, he was certain.

Jumping up from the floor he circled his magicks room to see if there was anything he would need on his journey. Nothing stood out to him, and so he strode to the door and came up short when he heard a knock.

Only two people had permission to knock on his magicks door.

"Mother," Callum said. He opened the door and leaned against the doorframe, looking down at his striking mother. She wasn't tall, and yet her very presence made everyone in the room feel small. With a flowing dress of red, pink curling hair, and violet eyes, Queen Aurelia looked stunning. As queen, she'd ruled with a fair and just hand, earning the respect of the nation and the hatred of every man who aspired to her throne. To those threats, she'd barely blinked an eye, and carried on with the business of running her kingdom.

Callum adored her.

"You're leaving." It wasn't a question. For a moment, her lips tightened as she pressed them together, before nodding once. "If you must go…"

"I must," Callum said. "I can't get her out of my head."

"Will you bring her back with you?"

"What? Of course I will. Is that what you were worried about?" Callum reached out to wrap an arm around his mother's shoulders.

"I didn't want to make assumptions about your plans."

"I don't have any plans other than to find her."

"And if she asks you to stay?"

"I'm hoping she'll be woman enough to compromise. At the very least so I can introduce her to our world and she can make a decision."

"She's human then." His mother met his eyes, and he couldn't read her thoughts.

"I believe so, yes."

"And you're comfortable with this?"

"Do I have a choice?" Callum let out a half-laugh and ran his hand through his hair.

"We all have choices, my child."

"What? To ignore her call? To try to find love with someone else?"

"You could live alone."

"Is that the life you want for me?" Callum whirled and stomped back into his room, going once more to his shelves. "To live alone and never mate?"

"I don't want that for you. I'm saying you have choices. You didn't ask me what I thought of her being a human."

"I already know. It would dilute the bloodline." Callum spit out.

"Oh, men." The queen laughed. "Always so concerned with details that don't really matter. It's why women make better rulers. You all get so focused on inconsequential matters when the thing that matters most is staring you right in the face."

"What's that?"

"Love, my dearest darling son. Love is all that matters. No power is greater. It doesn't matter to me if a human is your fated mate. It matters to me that you know love."

"But you just said I could live alone instead," Callum said.

"You can. It's a choice. I didn't say it was my choice for you. But it's a choice you have to make."

"If I don't go to her, I'll forever wonder what I missed out on. It will haunt me." Callum turned a pleading look at his mother.

"I think you'll know what is best to do."

"I do." Callum sighed and packed a few ingredients in a small leather satchel.

"You're going then?"

"Aye."

"Give her this, please. As a welcome gift. Perhaps it will ease her nerves before she arrives." The queen pulled a purple velvet bag from the folds of her dress.

"What is this?" Callum opened the bag and pulled out a stunning gold necklace of intricately knotted metal interspersed with pearls, all leading to a dramatic amethyst pendant wrapped in gold leaves. "It's beautiful."

"It's a gift from your father and me. She'll feel the love when she puts it on."

"First I must find her."

"I have faith you will. Be careful on your journey, my love. There's...something afoot."

"What do you mean by that?" Callum stopped beside the door and met his mother's violet eyes once more.

"The water fae are unhappy. I'll soothe them in time, but they have a right to be. Their home is being threatened and we must do what we can for them. I worry they'll revolt before I can make a change for them."

"Do they understand you are on their side?"

"I hope so. We'll see. Please be careful on your journey. Make smart decisions."

"I will do so. Thank you, for this," Callum held the bag up before tucking it in his leather satchel. "I hope to return with my bride."

"It will be good for the people to see you happy."

"Have I not been happy?"

"You've been you." The queen chuckled and nudged him to the door. "Go now, before the wind carries your secrets to those who wish you ill will."

"My love to you and Father. I will be in touch."

With that, Callum left and returned to his study, where he quickly changed into clothing charmed for seafaring, and gathered his things. Traveling lightly, with his bag, and a sword at his back and a knife at his waist, Callum returned to the portal and slipped through it, landing next to Nolan's small boat at the marina. His friend would forgive him for taking the boat, but not for embarking on his travels alone. However, Callum knew in his heart of hearts he must travel this journey on his own.

Unhooking the tiny boat from the dock, Callum whispered words of magick to carry the boat silently through the marina and at great speed, so that any of those who were looking would only see but a ripple on the water's surface. Only once far out into the sea, where the water fae began to pummel his boat and the bow bashed woefully against the waves, did Callum set his course.

He'd seen her walking the hills over Grace's Cove. When he'd called to her, his song on the wind, she'd turned and looked for him. She'd heard him. Of that, he was certain. Now, he only had to get to the cove. If only there were a portal near her, Callum would have slipped through the worlds quite easily. But there was too much magick in the cove for the fae to tamper with, which was why Callum now found himself being tossed about the ocean in this tiny boat.

"No matter. I'm coming for you, my love." Callum began to sing, and using magick, he propelled his boat through the water, bashing the water fae back as they tried to climb aboard and take control. His mother was right – the water fae *were* angry.

"Let me pass, my watery brethren. I mean no harm to you," Callum called, once again forcing one off his bow. "Please, I beg of you, don't make me hurt you."

"It's you we want. If we get you, the world will listen to our needs," one fae, bouncing up from the water, shrieked in his face, and Callum felt his stomach twist.

"Now is not the time. Please, be patient. We are on your side and we will help you save your home."

"Liar!" another fae shrieked.

"Faster," Callum urged the boat, picking up speed as the jagged cliffs of Grace's Cove appeared in the distance, spearing into the sky like two doors of a majestic gate. If he could just make it into the cove, he'd be safe and could find his fated mate.

It was the last wish he had before the fae succeeded in flipping his boat and dragging him under. Slippery hands gripped him and pulled him deeper. Panic threatened his magick as his mind raced to remember the words for a spell that might save him. In a last-ditch effort, Callum ran the spell before the fae pulled him deeper.

Larraim ort mo ghrá...

Chapter Six

QUEEN.

Lily snorted out a laugh and all but danced her way through the cottage. Oh, what a ridiculous night it had been – but at the same time, what fun! She'd stayed with Bianca and Seamus for hours, had herself three pints of cider, and had even hopped in on a round of dancing when the band in the front booth had kicked up a lively tune. Seamus and Bianca had been kind enough to drop her at her cottage, as apparently Seamus wasn't affected by the drink in the same way that she was.

Now, she was home – *her* home – and more than half tipsy. Mad with the delight of it all, Lily bounced around the room and pretended to make the chair in front of her curtsy.

"Queen Lily of the Fae," Lily said out loud, and laughed again. She could barely keep a class of toddlers in line, so she doubted running a kingdom of magickal beings – all whom had more power than her – would be an easy task. Seamus must be thinking of another Callum, for surely the man she dreamed about was just that – a dream.

Lily hummed the song from her dreams as she stood in front of her Christmas tree, wondering what it would be like to wake up on Christmas morning in the arms of her prince. Lily sighed and forced herself to accept she'd be alone for Christmas this year. No prince would be swooping through the doors to claim her for a mate.

But that didn't mean she couldn't write it. Clapping her hands together, she descended upon her leather notebook, stoked the fire, and curled up in the chair, letting the words come of their own accord. Before she knew it, the cider had its effect on her and her head dropped forward, and she slipped into sleep.

"Child, you must awaken."

"What…who?" Lily blinked her eyes open and looked wildly around before realizing she'd fallen asleep in her chair. "Who's there?"

"My name is Fiona." A woman with gray hair, kind whiskey-brown eyes, and a tumble of necklaces at her throat smiled over her. Lily squinted. It seemed as though…she could see through the woman? She must still be dreaming.

"Hi, Fiona. I'm Lily. Why are you visiting me in my dream?"

"You're not dreaming. I've awakened you from your slumber. Your man needs you."

"Excuse me?" Lily shot up, the notebook falling from her lap. She blinked her eyes in the dim light of the fire that had almost burned out. "I'm sorry…what is happening? Why are you even here?"

"I've walked these hills far longer than you, my dear. I'm one of Grace O'Malley's bloodline."

"You're a ghost."

"A spirit, yes. And I still visit here with family. Or, if I can reach a person, I let them know when trouble is afoot. And, well, trouble is afoot, my dear child."

"I'm sorry, I need a moment." Lily had no idea why she was apologizing to a ghost. She stood up and strode into the tiny kitchen, flipping on the light switch as she did. Keeping her back to Fiona, she filled a glass with water and drained it. A part of her hoped when she turned around that Fiona would no longer be standing there.

"Don't take too long, my dear. You'll lose him."

"Lose who? What are you saying to me?"

"Your mate needs your help."

"I don't have a mate. It's all just nonsense!" Lily shouted. Then she gasped and clasped her hands to her mouth. "I'm sorry, that was incredibly rude."

"I understand this is a lot to take in right now, but you're losing time. He needs you."

Lily looked at the ceiling of the cottage and took a deep breath, counting to ten. Did she believe this spirit that had appeared in her cottage?

"I'm...struggling."

"He's hurt. Badly. Now, you can sit here and struggle with whether you believe this is all happening or you can suspend disbelief for but a moment and go help the man who is about to give his life because he wanted to meet you."

At that, Lily slammed her water cup down. Bianca's words from earlier sprang to her mind. It *would* be bold of her to storm into the night and look for this supposed lover of hers. And, damn it, she wanted to be bold for once in her life.

"Okay, I believe you. Um, can you take me to him? What do I do? Do I call the doctor?"

"I will help you. He's at the cove. Go. Now."

Lily grabbed her coat and a flashlight she had put by the door. After jamming her feet into her waterproof boots, she trudged her way across the hills in the rain. Sliding when she lost her footing, stumbling, and half-laughing at the madness of it all, Lily fought the rain to finally land at the cliffs that overlooked the cove. Peering over the edge, she shone her flashlight down into the darkness.

"Damn it. I can't see anything," Lily said. She paused. It would be true insanity if she tried to navigate the narrow path down the cliff wall in the bracing winds that buffeted her back from the cliff's edge. All for what? She couldn't even see if someone was down there.

Lily gasped as the cove lit up from within, like it had earlier that day, a brilliant blue shining from the depths. She didn't even care what it meant at that point, for in its light she could see a body bent at a weird angle on the beach far below her.

"Oh, no, no, no," Lily said, and patted her pockets for a cell phone. Which she immediately discovered she'd left back at the cottage. Slapping a hand to her forehead, she turned to go back home to get help.

"Save him. You have very little time. The storm is growing worse," Fiona said.

Lily jolted and whirled on Fiona.

"I can't save him. I have nothing! I don't know how."

"I promised I would help you. Go to him. He needs you."

This had to be one of the most stupid things she'd done in her life, Lily thought, as she scrabbled her way down the path, hugging the cliff wall when gusts of wind threatened to tear her off the side. Tears dripped from her eyes, and her hands were scraped raw by the time she neared the bottom, but she persisted. Because the light never stopped glowing, and despite everything, Lily couldn't turn her back on someone who needed help.

When she finally reached the bottom of the path, she drew up short, shaking and soaked to the skin from the sheets of rain that battered her.

"I need an offering," Lily sobbed, patting her pockets. What could she give that meant anything at all? Her hands ran over the small bracelet on her wrist. A simple gold band with a mouse on it. Bruce had given it to her, back when she'd believed in his words, and she wore it now more out of habit than anything. Taking it off, Lily held it up to the waters that churned in the brilliant blue light.

"I mean you no harm. I only come here to help him." She tossed the bracelet into the water and waited for something to happen. When nothing did, she almost stomped her foot.

"That's really not fair, you know. You need to give a sign or something that you're not going to kill a person."

When no sign came, Lily gave up and raced for the body lying on the sand. Dropping to her knees at his side, she automatically reached for his pulse. When he turned his head slightly to look at her, Lily gasped.

It was Callum. The man of her dreams. Prince of Fae.

And he looked to be on his last breath.

"I called for you. My love."

"Oh, I heard you. I'm here," Lily said, grasping his hand.

"I'm…hurt. Badly. I don't know that…"

"Shhh. Don't talk. I'll figure out a way to help you. Save your energy. Please," Lily said. Turning, she looked for Fiona. "Damn it, woman. You'd said you'd help. What do I do? I am not strong enough to lift him out of here. He's dying!" she shrieked into the storm.

"Put your arms around him. I will join with you and you'll feel my power through you. Together, we'll bring him home."

Lily almost jumped a foot at the voice in her ear. Taking a few deep breaths, she settled herself and leaned over to slide her arms around Callum.

"Open to me," Fiona commanded.

Lily had no idea what that meant, but she did her best to picture her mind opening to Fiona's powers. Whatever she did seemed to work, because a power flooded her like a lilting spring breeze and she effortlessly cradled Callum at her chest.

"I can't believe…"

"Do not talk. Focus. This is tricky enough as it is."

"Right," Lily breathed, and began to half run, half walk her way across the beach to the path. Once there, she glanced up at the large climb ahead of her. Biting her lip, she looked down at Callum's ashen face and began to climb.

"Keep going. Love matters, Lily. You are strong enough for this," Fiona chanted over and over in Lily's head, and Lily took the mantra to heart, as she stepped foot after foot up the precarious path. Once at the top, she wanted to drop to her knees and weep.

"Not yet, dear love. Not yet."

"Home," Lily said. Taking a deep breath, she started for her cottage. It was quite a way from the cliffs, but with the storm at her back, it felt like the wind all but pushed them across the sodden fields. Never a happier sight greeted Lily's eyes than when she saw the kitchen light in her cottage shining through the damp darkness.

"Quickly now, we're losing him."

Lily stumbled her way to the door, awkwardly unlatching it and barely missing hitting Callum's head on the doorframe before she raced to the bedroom and deposited him on the bed.

"Now what? We need help! Where's my phone?" she cried, racing back across the room to dig in her purse. Pulling it out, she cried out once more. "Why is there never any signal out here?"

"Lily. Focus," Fiona ordered. Once more she stood across from Lily near the Fae Prince.

"I don't know how to focus because I don't know what to do."

"Open his pack and see what's in it. If he's a smart man, he'll have brought some magicks with him. We can work with that."

"I don't know how to do magick," Lily wailed.

"You're about to learn," Fiona said. She hovered over the table where Lily had dumped Callum's leather pack. "There. That bottle. The one that is faintly glowing purple, the gold bottle. It's a life elixir. Get it down his throat."

"Oh god, I hope this works." Lily ran to the bed and turned Callum's face to hers. Her heart hiccupped at the sight of him in real life, and the fact that he was struggling to take a breath made her want to scream.

"Tilt his head back. Open his mouth. Down the hatch."

"Yes, right. Okay." Lily did as she was told, pulling the little stopper from the gold bottle and upending it into his throat. When Callum began to sputter, she pinched his nose closed, which caused him to gasp and swallow the elixir. He dropped back to the bed.

"Now what?" Lily asked.

"Now you will strip him and tend to his wounds with a poultice I shall instruct you on making."

"You mean…get him naked?" Lily whispered, looking over her shoulder at Fiona in shock.

"Well, my dear, he's bleeding from a wound on his leg. What was your plan for that?"

"Is he?" Lily looked down and saw the blood seeping through his trousers. "Right. Strip him. Got it."

"It's for his best interest. Also, fae aren't shy. You won't be embarrassing him."

"Fae aren't shy," Lily said. She shook her head at the ridiculousness of it all, but managed to strip the clothes from Callum's body without too much fuss. Maybe she took a glance or two where she shouldn't, but it was purely to see if there were any injuries that needed tending. At least that's what she told herself.

When they'd identified the gravest wounds, Lily went to work at Fiona's instruction. "Are you certain we shouldn't seek medical care? Some of these seem quite deep?" Lily asked as she wound a bandage around

Callum's leg. Luckily, his breathing had evened out and he seemed to, at the very least, not be in immediate distress.

"How would you seek medical care? Your car is at the pub and your phone is out. Also, perhaps you don't recall the winter storm outside? Nobody will be going anywhere until this passes."

"But...what do I do?" Now that she wasn't in a full panic, Lily tuned into the sounds of the winds wailing over the little cottage.

"You've done all you can. Now his body needs rest to repair itself. Don't worry too much. The fae heal quickly. When the weather passes, I'll send Gracie to you if you still need healing help. She's not too far."

"Why did you not get her before now if she knows how to heal?"

When silence greeted her, Lily looked over her shoulder to see Fiona had left as quickly as she'd arrived.

"Oh, lovely. Just leaving me to it then. A schoolteacher with no medical training outside of basic first aid."

Lily sighed and dropped to the side of the bed. She'd covered Callum with a comforter, and now he looked as if he could be sleeping peacefully if she hadn't known any better. Lily studied the lines of his face, so sharp and regal against the cheerful quilt on the bed. She wanted to trace her hand over his face...to touch his lips.

The pull was so strong that her hand was halfway there before Lily caught herself. What was she doing? Instead, she grabbed some dry clothes and snuck to the bathroom for a steaming hot shower to try to work the cold from her bones. It felt like heaven and she never wanted to leave the safety of the shower, but knew she'd still have to face the man in her bed.

Once toweled off, Lily returned to the bed and hovered over Callum. His breathing continued to be even. Reaching out, she pressed a hand against the back of his forehead to check for fever. Lily gasped as his hand shot out and pulled her on top of him.

"No, you're hurt. I'll disturb your bandages…" Lily trailed off as his eyes slit open briefly.

"Don't leave me," Callum whispered. "Promise."

"I promise," Lily said, her heart catching as his lids dropped closed again.

And so Lily found herself curled up to a fae prince in the dead of the winter night during one of the worst storms Ireland had seen in ages.

Chapter Seven

SHE MUST STILL BE DREAMING, Lily thought, and turned, relaxing into the arms that wrapped around her. Tilting her head, she opened her lips for the kiss she craved.

Softly, at first, he explored her lips with almost reverence, sending delicious threads of heat curling through her body. Lily moaned against his mouth, craving more, delighting in the rightness of it. Only when he shifted, and a certain very male and very interested part of him pressed against her, did Lily gasp and pull back.

Callum's face slowly came into focus as Lily blinked her eyes and the events of last night came crashing back to her. Remembering that he was naked – and she was in bed with him – Lily squeaked and rolled from the bed to crouch on the floor.

"What are you doing down there?" Callum asked.

"You're real? Lily took a few shuddering breaths, her mind still crowded by lust from his kiss, and raised her head so just her eyes peered over the mattress at him.

"Of course I'm real. Did you think this was a dream?"

"Naturally. I've only ever met you in my dreams."

"That's fair, I suppose." Callum pursed his lips and studied her. "Shall I continue to converse while you hide on the floor or would you like to join me on the bed again?"

"I…hmm." Lily stood and skirted the end of the bed, and stood at a distance from Callum, her eyes drinking him in.

"You seemed much more welcoming a few minutes ago," Callum commented. He stretched back in bed, making no move to get out from under the covers, and crossed his arms behind his head.

Lily gulped as muscles rippled across his bare chest. There was something about the cheerful and fussy quilt that was making him look even more masculine than she had previously imagined. Or perhaps it was the taste of his kiss on her lips.

"Yes, well, I was still sleeping."

"I like sleeping Lily. She welcomes me in her dreams."

"Sure, and she's just a figment of your imagination."

"Is she? Why?" Callum studied her as closely as she was studying him. The pull to go to him was strong, and she briefly wondered if she'd been put under a spell of sorts.

"Dream Lily is a fierce warrior. Daytime Lily is…well, she's a work in progress."

"I think you're very fierce. You saved my life, didn't you?"

"Well, not on my own. I had help."

"Don't downplay it. Not many women would have

raced into a storm to save a man they'd only met in their dreams. It's very brave, and commendable. If you were one of my soldiers, I'd award you a medal."

"You would?" The thought charmed Lily. A medal of her own.

"I can have one made for you. If it pleases you."

"I think it would," Lily admitted, and took one step closer. "How…how are you feeling?"

"Better. I'll need at least another day to heal, and it's lucky I am that you found my life elixir."

"Well, I had help. Honestly…" Lily clapped her hands in an awkward little movement. "I have no idea what I'm doing. I have no idea if this is even real. I'm still…"

"Adjusting?"

"Yes, that's a grand word for it."

"We have the rest of our lives for you to adjust. So take your time."

"The rest of our…" Lily blew out a breath. "I feel like there's a lot that I need to be caught up on before I'm promising anyone the rest of my life."

"You don't feel it?"

"Feel what?"

"This?" Callum pointed between them both. "This draw? The power? The connection?"

"Oh, I thought maybe you'd put a spell on me."

At that, Callum threw back his head and laughed. His laughter turned into a bout of coughing, and Lily scurried into the kitchen for a glass of water. Returning to the bedroom, she handed it to a grateful Callum.

"Aye, I'll be needing a lot of this. The damn water fae tried to kill me. Mother will not be happy with this news."

"Water fae?" Lily wrung her hands together.

"Aye, they can be friendly as all get out. Or wee nasty beasties."

"Wee beasties. Water fae. Right," Lily said, feeling like her mind couldn't keep up with all the information being tossed at her.

"Lily." Callum smiled and beckoned her closer. She went, because it was impossible to resist him, and sat gingerly on the edge of the bed next to him.

"Yes?"

"We're fated mates, you and me. It's not a spell that can be made and not a spell that can be undone. It just is."

"Oh," Lily said. Her eyes widened as she drank him in, loving his nearness, her heart hammering in her chest.

"*Oh*, the lass says." Callum chuckled. "You really do need some time to adjust, don't you?"

"I didn't think you were real. It's like a figment of my imagination just walked through the door. I'm…processing."

"We'll take it slow then. The good thing is, we won't be going anywhere for a while and we won't be having any visitors either."

"Really? Why is that?"

Callum smiled again, sending heat through her, and nodded toward the window. "You don't hear the storm?"

"Right, of course, the storm," Lily said. The wind had been howling for so long now it was almost as if she'd just tuned it out to focus on more important things in her life. Like the fact that a supposed Fae Prince sat naked in her bed.

"It's the water fae. They've kicked up a right fit now

that they've lost me. I was lucky to get my magick around me before they took me completely under."

"The water fae are causing the storm?"

"Yes, a right nasty one too. I suspect we'll be here for several days. Which is good, because I'm sensing you are going to need a lot of time to acclimate to my presence. Though...maybe sleeping Lily will let me close." Callum winked at her, and Lily lost her breath and her train of thought for a moment. She was surprised to find herself leaning in for a kiss. Snapping back, she blushed.

"I'm sorry about that, I have no idea what's come over me."

"It's our soul connection. You're my fated mate. We'll always feel this draw to each other. You can't deny it."

"I think...I think I need a moment to ground myself," Lily said. She stood and looked down at him, but tempered her words with a smile. "It's silly, I know. But when I get a bit anxious, I need to back up and ground myself in a few things I can focus on that I know to be real."

"It's not silly. It sounds like a smart mechanism."

"Um, thank you. So, what I'm going to do is go to the kitchen and get an idea of how much food we have and maybe put some breakfast together. Oh...wait. Do you eat food?"

Callum threw his head back and laughed again, seemingly delighted with her, and Lily felt heat flood her cheeks again. "Of course I eat food, my love. But thank you for checking with me first. It's very considerate of you."

"Well, I didn't know. You could eat clouds or something for all I know about the fae." Lily turned, feeling unaccountably grumpy, and started to move to the kitchen, only to be caught up short when Callum grabbed her arm.

"I wasn't making fun of you. I just thought it was a funny question. Of course you wouldn't know what we eat. I was charmed by you, not having a laugh at your expense."

"Thank you for your explanation." Lily blew out a breath. "I'm a bit touchy right now, is all. Let me just… yes, just let me calm myself a bit and we'll go from there."

"Of course. I'll be right here, waiting for you to grace me with your presence."

Lily just nodded and left the bedroom, plopping into a chair at the little kitchen table. For a moment, she just put her head in her hands and took a moment to breathe. This all was actually happening. Nobody could have a dream that lasted this long. She needed to ground herself and maybe see if she could double check what was reality.

Leaning over, she grabbed her iPhone where it was plugged into the wall and rolled her eyes at the lack of signal. Turning, she scanned the cottage. There was a little television in the corner, but she'd never once used it since she'd arrived. Wondering if she could get any public access channels, Lily flipped it on, but only a fuzzy screen of static greeted her.

"The radio." Lily turned to the tiny transistor radio by the sink. She had used it a few times while cleaning the house and had been pleased to get a few local radio stations through. Flicking it on, she pushed open a shutter on one of the windows to peer outside into the morning.

Brace yourselves, Ireland…this storm is one for the books. Particularly affected will be the west coast. Author-

ities are recommending that everyone stay home unless for emergencies. And, no, needing a pint at the pub is not an emergency. Keep the roads clear for medical personnel.

"So, that holds up…" As did the weather outside. Lily struggled with slamming the shutter back closed after the wind threatened to take it clear off the side of the house. From her small glimpse of the outside, it could still be night for how dim it was. Angry gray clouds battled in the sky, and the wind howled in agony, battering the cottage with sharp shards of rain and ice. No, they weren't going anywhere so long as this held up.

Now, what to do with the handsome man in her bed? One idea popped in her head, but Lily shoved that thought aside. She didn't know this man and she still didn't know if she could believe he was the fae prince from her dreams. Perhaps there was some other explanation. Maybe she had some sort of precognition that had never developed until Bruce had hit her? Or maybe he'd hit her harder than she'd realized and she had brain damage?

Sighing, Lily rubbed her hands over her face. It was good to question things, but right now she had no real answers and no way to test reality.

She could only go with her heart.

And wasn't that a scary prospect, Lily mused, opening her cupboard doors. She had to trust herself and her instincts in how she navigated the steps forward.

Basic needs first, Lily told herself, and forced her mind to focus. She took stock of the cupboard, relieved she'd seen fit to buy a lot of the basics like baking supplies, cans of soup, and a few other pantry staples. In the small fridge, she had milk, cream, butter, some vegetables, and two weeks' worth of eggs. It wouldn't be fancy food, but enough to feed them for a few days. She'd even tucked a bottle of whiskey and a few bottles of wine in her shopping cart, and was glad to have them now.

The wind slapped at the house, causing the shutters to rattle, and thunder rolled overhead. If this really was the water fae causing the storm – and that was a big *if* – it made Lily nervous to know she was housing the target of their fury.

Not wanting to be away from Callum much longer, she decided to go with a simple breakfast of porridge and tea. Carrying in the tray of food to the bedroom, Lily paused when she saw Callum's eyes closed. She was about to turn when they slit open again and he smiled.

"I was just doing my own grounding. Healing takes a lot of energy."

"You're looking remarkably better than last night. I was certain you'd died."

"I was close. Closer than my mother will forgive the water fae for. They've started a nasty battle, that's for sure."

"Okay, I have so many questions," Lily laughed. "But first, let me put this tray down and pull this little table and chair over. We can have some food to get our strength back. And then, depending on how you feel, maybe you'll be open to telling me more?"

"I'll tell you anything, my love. I have no secrets from you."

The words warmed her heart, for Bruce had always kept secrets from her, but still, she needed to get a grip here before she flung herself into bed and had her way with an injured man who thought he was a Fae Prince. Instead she nudged the bowl toward him and they both dipped into their porridge while the storm raged outside.

In any other respect, it would have been a cozy morning. If only Lily could convince herself that she wasn't going mad.

Chapter Eight

"YOU'RE lovely when you're thinking. Well, you're lovely all the time. But particularly when you are worrying on a wee problem. I can see your brain turning over behind those gorgeous eyes of yours."

Lily looked up from her porridge bowl, caught on his words. "Really?"

"Aye, really. It's taking all my power not to toss that table aside and pull you into bed with me."

"Really?" Lily breathed again, and was shocked to find that she was definitely in favor of that course of action. What was wrong with her? She'd never had this reaction to someone before.

"You find this surprising?" Callum chuckled and put his empty bowl on the side table. "The only thing that surprises me is that there isn't a line of suitors outside your door."

"Oh, that's not surprising," Lily said. She dropped her gaze back to the porridge bowl, heat tinging her cheeks with embarrassment. A man like Callum likely had a long history of lovers in his past, what with his silvery hair, dark eyes, and a body cut from granite. It was likely women threw themselves at him.

Bruce had been her first and only boyfriend. There hadn't been anyone else who had expressed a particular interest in her. That she was aware of, anyway.

Lily sighed. She needed to work on building herself up more and less internal beratement. It was a promise she'd made to herself in the last few weeks, but she was learning what a difficult habit it was to break.

"Why would you say that? Any man would be lucky to have you by their side. I'd kill them, of course, but still..." Callum mused.

Lily's eyes shot to Callum's and her mouth dropped open. "You'd kill them? Why?"

"For touching my woman, of course. But that's neither here nor there. Tell me why you think you aren't lovely. I simply can't understand such thoughts. You're positively ethereal. I shiver just being in your presence."

"You do?" Lily gasped. A smile, unbidden, stretched across her lips and warmth filled her soul.

"Naturally. Lily, you're breathtaking. But I fear you've been hurt. This is not normal for a woman so lovely to be so shy. Will you tell me who has dimmed your light?"

"Dimmed my light..." Lily said, rolling the words over in her brain. It was such an interesting and thoughtful way to encapsulate her experiences. He wasn't wrong, at that. Bruce *had* dimmed her light. But he'd certainly not shut it off. It was this light that propelled her through the night to save Callum, she reminded herself, and what would allow her to open herself to a man she had only known in her dreams.

"Yes. I'm sorry if those words hurt you."

"No, they didn't hurt me." But the fact that he cared about her feelings made Lily feel calmer inside. "I was in a difficult relationship."

"He hurt you." It wasn't a question, and something quivered in Lily when she saw the fierce light flash into Callum's eyes.

"No, no, no…" Lily began, but then she made herself pause. If this man was truly her fated mate or whatever he called it, she shouldn't lie to him. And if this was all a figment of her imagination, then it didn't really matter if she told the truth. There was nobody who could hurt her now but herself. She was done covering for Bruce. "Actually, that's not true."

"He did hurt you. Where is he? Who is this man? I will destroy him."

Though Lily was secretly thrilled by Callum coming to her defense with no explanation, she held up her hand to stop his words. Violence wasn't the energy she wanted to put out into the world. "If I tell you, you must promise to not hurt him."

"Absolutely not," Callum seethed.

"You must. It's not…it won't help me heal to see him hurting."

"You won't see him hurting if he is dead. There will be no pain," Callum said matter-of-factly.

"Oh…right. Okay, no murdering. That's certainly frowned upon in this world."

"Humans can be such delicate creatures." Callum

patted the bed next to him. "Will you come sit by me and tell me about the man who hurt you? I will promise not to kill him, but secretly wish I could."

"I suppose I can do that if you make me another promise."

"What's that?"

"That you won't touch me until I'm ready."

Callum's eyes flashed with a different kind of heat this time, and Lily felt her insides go liquid. He could have her with but a look, she realized, and pressed her lips together as she held onto a tenuous thread of control.

"Of course, my queen. Perhaps I'll even wait until you beg?"

"Oh..." Lily's mind seemed to short circuit for a moment, and it took her several deep breaths before she remembered what she had asked. "I will ask when I am ready."

There, that sounded mature, Lily thought, and then stood and tripped over the table, immediately plummeting onto the bed, her face landing about two inches from an area she had just been trying very hard not to focus on. Lily struggled for a moment, rolling around on Callum's legs like a turtle flipped on its back before she was able to get purchase and scramble to the other side of the bed.

"I would have helped you, but you'd just asked me not to touch you," Callum supplied helpfully, and Lily was certain she'd blushed all the way down to her toes.

"And this would be why I don't have men lining up at my door." She buried her face in her hands.

"I can guarantee you that many men would be more than delighted to have you land facedown in their lap."

"Oh, stop it!" Lily said, but despite her embarrassment she felt a laugh bubble up. "I can be a tad clumsy at times."

"I have no problem with that. Well, when you allow me to touch you, that is. Every man likes to save his woman when he can."

"I'm not...this isn't..." Lily wrung her hands. "Let's back up."

"Would you like some tea?" Callum didn't wait for an answer, but poured her a fresh cup from the pot on his table. "Here, drink this and tell me about the man I'm not supposed to kill."

"Right, okay." Lily took a sip of tea and then leaned back against the pillows as she thought about her words. The storm continued to rage across the hills, but it was cozy inside, curled on the bed with Callum, and she felt the tea soothe her angst as she thought about her past.

"Maybe it is easier to start with telling me more about yourself? Where did you grow up?"

"Oh, sure, that's a bit easier. I grew up outside Dublin. A small community by the water. It was just me and my mum. She's off in Scotland now, but I see her on holidays."

"No father?"

"No, he passed when I was only a baby. My mum always wanted to remarry, and went through a slew of partners after she lost my father. I think she was trying to fill the hole he left in her heart. Grief is tough, I guess. She was a good mum, just...fanciful. I suppose that's where I get all my daydreaming from. It is easier to get lost in dreams than it is in reality."

"I'm grateful for my dreams because it's where I met you."

"How can you be so certain of us?" Lily slanted Callum a look. "You say this as if we are a foregone conclusion. It's...mind boggling."

"I feel it." Callum touched a hand to his heart. "Don't you have fated mates among humans?"

"Um, I suppose some people feel there are soul mates. But it's not something that compels you to be with someone or calls to you across the lands."

"Soul mates." Callum rolled the words around on his tongue. "I like the sound of that."

"I struggle with the concept myself, as my mum was always finding a new soul mate. Every new boyfriend was her next soul mate."

"Lust can often be confused for love."

"Or loneliness," Lily said. She plucked at a loose thread in the blanket.

"Were you lonely, sweet Lily?"

"I was. I am, I guess. But maybe not so much anymore. I think I've learned to be comfortable without many friends and that sort of thing."

"Because of this man."

"Yes, I suppose so. And, well, I'm shy and can feel overwhelmed at social gatherings, so I often hug the corners. I don't make connections as easily as others, really."

"There's nothing wrong with that, Lily. A cautious approach to friendships can be considered a wise one."

"Yes, well, I should have been more cautious in picking my first boyfriend."

"This man? He was your first and only then?"

"Yes." Lily looked down at the comforter.

"Thankfully, I only have one man to kill then."

"Hey! I said no violence."

"Fine. Continue your story." Callum rolled to his side and propped his head on his hand. Lily lost her train of thought for a moment as she ogled his muscular chest. "You've only to ask to touch me, Lily."

"Oh! I'm sorry, I shouldn't stare." She tore her eyes away. "Back to the story, which really isn't all that exciting. He was very charming. I met him at the school I worked at. He was the activities coach."

"Activities coach?"

"Sports, exercise…that kind of thing."

"Ah. Go on." Callum shifted, and Lily tried not to glance at him to see if the blanket stayed in place.

"He was very charismatic. I'd never had someone like him show interest in me before. I admit, I got a bit swept up in the attention he gave me. Before I knew it, we were a couple and my whole life became focused on one thing."

"Him?"

"Correct. His happiness became number one. I didn't realize it, not at first. I was just so pleased to be included for once, you understand? We were invited to parties and the other teachers were more friendly at school. For a while…well, it *was* nice."

"But this changed."

"It did. I mean, it was my fault…" Lily stopped herself. "Wait, no. Let me back up. I'm working on this."

"On what?"

"I've been reading a self-help book on how to recover

from an abusive relationship. And one of the things they say is to not take blame for…" Lily trailed off as Callum whipped the blanket off and jumped up, standing very naked and very angry in front of her.

"Where is this man? I rescind my promise to you. I will kill him."

"You…wait…no…"

"Tell me where he is. I will find the one who hurt you."

"I don't want you to find him. I just got away from him."

"I will make him bleed."

"No…really, it's fine. I left. I'm okay." Lily patted the bed and nervously averted her eyes. "Please get under the covers, I can't think when you're standing there with no clothes on." She waited until the bed dipped beside her and there was a tugging motion on the cover.

"I'm covered."

"To be clear – he only hit me once."

Callum hissed softly.

"And I left right after because I knew it would get worse. But the abuse I'm talking about is deeper, it's more ingrained. It's years of someone making you feel small, making you feel like everything you do is wrong, making you feel like you can't trust your own choices. Do you understand?"

"I don't, because I have never been in the situation. But I can empathize."

"I'll accept that. Thank you for the honest answer." Lily gave Callum a small smile and hugged her knees to her chest. "I realize now that I let him take charge of my life until I was basically at his beck and call."

"You didn't let him. He took that from you."

Lily dipped her head in acknowledgement. "Also something I am working on. I have to work on not taking blame for things that aren't my own actions."

"I'll help you."

It was a simple statement, and yet…it made Lily want to cry from the sweetness of it. He wanted her to better herself – for her. It was such a simple and yet alien concept for her from a man. A *partner*. Could Callum really be her partner?

"You're very kind, Callum."

"Not all would agree with you."

"You're being very kind to me, then. I suppose you have to be harsh at times when you rule. Oh! I have so many questions."

"When we finish your story, I will tell you mine."

"That's fair. There isn't much more." Lily took another sip of her tea as she thought about it. "I pretty much was living on autopilot. I dreamed at night, and I had silly daydreams of becoming a writer one day. But otherwise, my life just kind of plodded along until Bruce's fists snapped me out of my daze."

Callum hissed again but said nothing.

"And I left. That night while he was sleeping. I'd packed a bag before…sort of my emergency 'get out of town' bag. In case…well, in case I ever could work up the courage to go. I think I'd known for a lot longer than I'd realized that I needed to leave. I guess I needed to see the worst of it before I could bring myself to do it. I don't know why either. Isn't that silly? If I wasn't happy – why didn't I just leave before?"

"Sometimes hope can be a dangerous thing."

"You're absolutely right. I think I kept hoping things would be different. I dreamed of different realities. I tried to change and cater to his needs, but ultimately, nothing I did made him happy. And that was when I had to leave."

"You are the Lily of my dreams."

"What?" She looked at him over her teacup.

"You. You're not daytime Lily. You're fierce warrior Lily."

"Not…no, not really," she laughed.

"Yes, you are. Did you know anyone in this town when you came here? Did you leave in the dead of the night and just go?"

"I did. Actually, yes, I did. I went to the airport to rent a car and drove across Ireland."

"In the middle of the night. Now you've got yourself a lovely cottage and a new life. And when someone told you that a person was hurt in the middle of a winter storm, you ran to them. Against all odds, you found and saved me. You, my sweet and fierce Lily, are a warrior goddess."

"Oh…" Tears pricked Lily's eyes and she buried her face in her teacup while she struggled to hang onto her composure. She wasn't a pretty crier and certainly didn't need to be a snotty mess all over Callum.

"Be at peace, Lily. You may leave your demons behind. I've got you now," Callum said. Lily turned to see his hand inches from her arm, respecting her space. His eyelids drooped, and she realized just how tired he still must be. The poor man was healing from a very traumatic injury and here she was unloading her life problems on him.

"I'll accept your protection," Lily whispered to the softly snoring Callum, and threaded her fingers through his on the comforter. "Even if it's just for this moment."

Chapter Nine

HE SLEPT most of the day, and Lily didn't dare wake him, because in her opinion sleep was the best thing for anyone's health. She spent a lovely afternoon humming softly to herself while she baked cinnamon scones and soda bread, and put together ingredients for a vegetable stew for dinner. The storm continued to batter the small cottage, and there were a few moments Lily was half-convinced the winds would just pick the cottage up and toss it across the hills.

Now she enjoyed a small glass of whiskey by the fire and had pulled her leather notebook out. There had been no more visits from Fiona and no other way to contact the outside world. Not that there was much need, as there wasn't much to do but wait out the storm and make sure Callum healed properly. Instead of writing, though, Lily found herself staring into the fire.

He'd seen her.

Callum had really looked at her. He could see her struggles, and hadn't made her feel worse for them.

Instead, he'd championed her decisions and had promised his support. It was…a novel idea, at that. Was this what a true partnership would look like? Lily tried to imagine herself holding court among the Fae, draped on Callum's arm and covered in jewels, and laughed at herself.

"What's brought a smile to that lovely face?"

"Oh!" Lily almost dropped her whiskey, but saved it in time. "You startled me. How are you feeling?"

"Much better, thank you. Ravenous, I'll admit."

"I don't doubt it. You slept all day. I've made food if you'd like to join me for dinner."

"I'd love to. Can I help?"

"Um, if you could maybe…find a sheet to wrap around you?" Lily blushed and looked away. Fiona hadn't been kidding when she said the fae were comfortable with nudity.

"Do you not like my form?"

"No, I mean, yes, of course, it's very nice," Lily said. "It's just…distracting."

"Ah, you like to look?"

"Of course – I mean, you're beautiful. But also I don't think I could eat with you naked at the table."

"What if I eat naked in that chair?" Callum leaned against the doorframe and pointed to the chair across from her.

"Also would be distracting."

"I bet you are also beautiful with no clothes. You have a lovely shape," Callum said.

"Right. Um. Thank you. Now, go. Sheet. In the drawer." Lily glanced at her cup and took the rest of the whiskey down in one gulp. It screamed its way down her throat, but also forced her to pull her mind away from all of the delicious thoughts now dancing through her brain. Letting out a breath, she stood and turned to go to the kitchen.

"Better?" Callum stood in the doorway once again, this time with a white sheet wrapped low around his hips and a devilish smile on his handsome face. The firelight caught the edges of his face, his eyes alight with mischief, and for a moment he looked every inch a dangerous rogue. The most surprising bit was that for the first time Lily felt herself wanting to walk into danger instead of running from it.

"You look like walking sex, but yes, better." She smiled when Callum threw his head back and laughed.

"I aim to please."

"Yes, well. Hmmm. So, dinner." Lily infused her tone with a brightness and moved to the kitchen, where her stew was simmering on the stove. "I made a vegetable stew and I have soda bread and scones. Will that do?"

"Of course, it smells wonderful. Maybe a bottle of wine?" Lily turned to find Callum nosing in her cupboards. Wine, dinner, and a half-naked man was not a date Lily thought she would be having anytime soon, but here she was. Maybe the wine would loosen his tongue and she'd get some answers from him about all this fae business. Aside from Fiona showing up as a ghost, Lily had yet to see anything magickal about this man.

Well, aside from what the sheet now covered.

"Wine would be lovely, thank you," Lily trilled. She turned back to the stove and ladled the soup into chunky blue bowls. When she turned back, she almost dropped the soup all over herself. "Callum! What is this?"

"I set the table for dinner?" Callum looked at her with a questioning look on his handsome face.

The plain wooden dinner table now sported a shimmering green tablecloth, vibrant purple napkins, and dishware made of gold. A gold vase held wildflowers, and two tapered pillar candles sat on either side of it.

"Was…this stuff here?" Lily asked, though she already knew the answer.

"No, I conjured it."

"With your magick."

"Correct."

"Oh…kay. This is going to take some getting used to."

"You don't like it?" Worry crossed Callum's face.

"No, I didn't say that. I'm just…well, I'm still questioning whether I'm dreaming or not," Lily said. She put the bowls on the table and slid into a chair, her mind whirling at the beautiful craftsmanship of the gold wineglasses. "It's still hard to know what's real."

"This is real," Callum said. He crouched by her side, but didn't touch her. "We are real. We just come from different lands."

"And you're okay with that? I mean, I'm nonmagickal. Surely you must marry a magickal fae for your bloodline." Oops. She'd just brought up marriage. That was one way to ruin a first date.

"I'm meant for my fated mate. And that, my love, is you. Now, I'll admit, I have felt it was best to keep human and fae apart."

"Why is that?" Lily watched as Callum moved around

the table and gracefully sat in his chair. She waited as he poured them both a glass of wine.

"Because I think that we are very different and too much blending will harm both humans and fae. I think we have a healthy balance of intermixing, at the moment. If we opened to more, well, it could cause great harm to your people due to my people's magicks."

"But not the other way around?" Lily took a sip of her wine.

"Fae have more power than humans. We are endlessly enchanted and amused by the antics of humans, but I fear more would end up hurt than cherished by fae. Some fae don't have an off switch when it comes to pleasure."

"You mean they'd rape them?"

Callum shot her a horrified look. "No, I mean they would take and take…be it whatever was amusing them. It could be a musician with a beautiful voice. They could enchant the person to sing forever for them…and steal their free will. They may not even realize they are doing it. We're used to having our needs met."

"Oh. I don't think I like the sound of that." Lily took a spoonful of her soup and blew on it. "I think free will is very important."

"As do I. Which is why until I know for sure the fae wouldn't cause great harm to the humans, I've generally supported rulings that impose restrictions on how they interact."

"And now? Say we really are fated mates? What will your people think?"

"They'll have opinions, I'm certain of it. However, most will be happy for me. And for us. You see, a fated mate is deeply honored in our culture. It's just...understood. And, if you are lucky enough to not only have one, but find them? It's applauded."

"Not everyone has a mate?" Lily asked. "That's...well, that sounds sad."

"It doesn't mean they are lonely. It just means they won't know great love. They can still love, live their lives, and find contentment. It's a different life, is all."

"I really have so many questions." Lily leaned forward. "Like...what is it like in your world? How do you get from your world to here? What was it like growing up as a prince? Will you be king someday? How does your magick work? How many factions of fae are there? You mentioned water fae. Are there others? What about..."

Callum held up his hand and she stopped, laughing at herself. "I will try to answer these questions first before you add more. Let's see...in my world we are a joyful people. We like to celebrate all things, and we are always up for some sort of entertainment. Magick, music, lovers...they all flow easily. However, we can be a violent society when pushed to protect our loves. You see, protecting those we love is one of the greatest acts of service we can provide. We even have a faction of protectors dedicated to protecting humans who have certain quests to fulfill for us or certain fae-like traits."

"Protectors." He'd promised to protect her last night. In a certain amount of words, at least.

"Aye, protectors. As I will now be yours." Callum smiled lazily at Lily.

"You're my protector."

"Yes." Callum took a bite of his soda bread. "This is delicious."

"Wait, so protect me from what, exactly?"

"Those who mean you harm. Including yourself."

"Myself? I wouldn't self-harm."

"Your words do."

Add that to her self-reflection pile, Lily thought, and took a piece of soda bread.

"To answer your other questions…we travel to your world through portals that are monitored by our security personnel. Growing up as a prince was interesting, because I started my magickal work sooner than most and was tasked with harder challenges in order to make my powers grow. However, I have very doting parents who were both tough and loving in the same breath. I wasn't spoiled, but I was and am privileged. Yes, I will be king someday, but not for a while.

"There are many factions of fae in varying levels of magic. Water fae, woodland fae, fire fae…those are all elemental type fae. All magickal and strong in their own right, however." Callum nodded to the window, where the storm continued to scream its wrath. "Though our people are stronger. We try not to war with the other fae as our people believe it is in Earth's best interests to live harmoniously. It's also why we've kept a border between humans. Unfortunately, not all humans would treat us as justly as most of us treat them."

"But you just said that some fae would be intoxicated with humans and push them to their limits."

"Some. Not all. I'd rather not find out how many."

"The same could be said for humans, then."

"I agree. It's why we've erred on the side of caution instead of mingling the worlds. Risk to reward, my love."

"And yet, here you are."

"You called to me," Callum said. He reached his hand across the table but stopped short before touching her fingers. "I had to come to you."

"I want to believe this," Lily whispered, meeting his eyes, as an almost tangible cord of emotion pulled her to lean closer to him. "I really want this to be true and not some insane dream."

"Do you want to see more magick? It seems like this is an area that confuses you."

"I would. I don't understand how magick works. And I've never really seen it, and they say seeing is believing…"

"Who is this *they*?" Callum demanded.

"You know, it's just…it's a saying," Lily laughed and drank more of her wine.

"What kind of magick would you like?"

"I have no idea how to respond to that." Lily leaned back in her chair and studied Callum. "Can you just do anything you want?"

"Of course not. Some spells are much bigger than others. Like the life elixir you gave me? That takes months to prepare. It is some of our greatest magick and must be used sparingly."

"Oh no!" Lily said, "I gave you the full bottle."

"I needed the full bottle."

"Then…you're welcome," Lily decided, and finished her wine.

"Thank you for saving my life, Lily. Would you like to see some magick?"

"I would."

"Hmm, where to start…" Callum tapped his lips and leaned back in his chair, and Lily lost herself for a moment just looking at him. He looked like a fallen angel, wrapped in white, with the muscles of a Greek statue. She gasped when he lifted his hand and a little flash of light surrounded it. The light disappeared as quickly as it had come, and in his hand remained a small gold circle.

"What is it?"

"For you, my love." Callum passed her the medallion. She took it and smiled at the design. Her face was intricately carved into the gold and beneath it was the word *Heroine*.

"A medal?" Lily asked in delight.

"For honor. Thank you for being my heroine."

"I will treasure it always." Lily laughed and pressed it to her heart. "I've never earned a medal before."

"Well, you've earned one now, and likely the undying devotion of my entire family, if not most of the fae world."

"Seriously?" Lily's eyes widened. The fae world was sounding increasingly enthralling.

"Seriously. Since you seem to like the gold…how about this?" Callum held his hands up, and Lily almost jumped out of her chair as gold sparkles began to rain down from the ceiling. It was like watching a gentle snowfall, but with gold flecks instead.

"How are you doing this?" she asked, catching some gold in her hand. They didn't dissolve like snow, and were warm to the touch.

"Magick is quite simply accessing universal energy. I pulled one element through another."

"Uh-huh," Lily said, watching the gold shower. "You make it sound easy."

"It is when you've learned from the greatest teachers."

"This is incredible. I think I'm finally beginning to believe you're really real."

"Thank you, I think?" Callum said, and Lily laughed at the look on his face.

"This is just all so far out from the world I was living. You'll have to give me time to get up to speed."

"I understand. Perhaps we can sit by the fire and talk some more?"

"I'd like that," Lily agreed. She stood and then halted when the gold winked from sight. Looking around, she didn't see any on the floor or anywhere. At least she wouldn't have to clean it up, she thought. Because there was no way she would let gold flecks sit around her house and not bottle them up for safekeeping.

"Leave the dishes. I will clean them," Callum said.

"Oh, but it will only take a moment…" Lily trailed off as the dishes appeared, cleaned and stacked nicely by the sink.

"Now you will join me?" Callum asked.

"I can see where magick can be handy," Lily said. Turning, she joined Callum by the fire, where he'd settled into a chair.

"What is this?" Callum said, paging through her leather notebook.

"Oh! Wait, no, it's private…" Lily trailed off as Callum looked up, heat in his eyes.

"This has my name in it."

"Yes, well, I dreamed of you."

"These are your dreams?" Callum asked, holding up her leather book.

"No, not all of them. Some of them are stories I am making up. I…" Lily lowered herself to the chair, her heart thumping in her chest as he read her words. "I have a secret dream of being a writer. I want to write fairy tales."

"Lily! That's wonderful! Writers are very much revered in our world." Callum beamed at her. "I am particularly enjoying this passage about when the warrior goddess meets me in the tower late one night. This is not so shy, Lily."

"No," she gulped, her throat dry, "it's not."

"Perhaps you will let me give this to you?"

"Give…what?" Lily felt like the room had gotten very warm.

"This moment. I have a tower. I can give this to you. I would enjoy this very much."

"Maybe…in time," Lily said, feeling a little light-headed at the thought of what she had written about this man.

"You are not ready for my touch."

"I'm…wow. You are very direct," she said, and Callum laughed.

"Love should be celebrated. There is no shame in having needs."

"I'm feeling a little overwhelmed," she admitted.

"Will you sleep next to me? This night? We can dreamwalk together and I will make you more comfortable. I want you to know that I love you."

Lily's heart tripped and she leaned forward, tugged by their invisible connection, and just looked at him. "How can you possibly know you love me?"

"Because I know you from my dreams. And I know you now. And I trust what is here." Callum held a hand to his heart. "This is right. And I know you feel it too. But I understand why you hesitate to say it back."

"I'm not…"

"You're not ready. But I have a lifetime to show you. So, for tonight, will you sleep next to me and dreamwalk with me?"

Lily took a deep breath and listened to her heart.

"Yes, Callum. I'd love nothing more."

Chapter Ten

SHYNESS CREPT over Lily as she approached the bed. She'd pulled on a tank and sleep pants – nothing revealing – and had left her hair to tumble down her back. Callum lay in his spot in bed, the covers thankfully pulled over him, and smiled at her approach.

"I like your sleep pants. Though you need more color."

"More color? What's wrong with these?" Lily looked down at her pale pink tartan flannel bottoms.

"May I?" Callum asked, and Lily just shrugged. A shiver of cool air crept over her body and then she gasped as she looked down at herself. A deep purple satin sleep gown flowed over her skin. She turned and looked at herself in the mirror, wondering where her other clothes had gone.

"How did you…where are…?" Lily gaped at herself.

"Look at this color on you. It's rich and vibrant, like yourself. Look how it brings out those beautiful eyes of yours. A color fit for a queen. My queen."

Lily studied herself, trying to see herself through his

eyes. He'd given her modesty in this gown, with nothing too low-cut or sexy, and yet the material was everything. It slid over her body, and its shimmer and movement was more sensual than if she'd worn nothing at all to bed. He was right, she realized, purple did marvelous things for her complexion, and her eyes looked...was that a come-hither look? Lily almost laughed at that thought, but reminded herself not to be mean. She could be come-hither if she *wanted* to be come-hither.

"I don't know why I've never worn purple before."

"You dress like you want to hide. As though you don't want people to notice you."

"Do I? I don't think I've ever realized that."

"I saw it when I dreamwalked with you. I was itching to take off that last shapeless gray dress you wore. You deserve color and fun."

Lily rounded the bed, enjoying how the satin slipped over her skin, and got into bed next to Callum. Tilting her head up, she met his eyes. "You're absolutely right, Callum. I do deserve more. Thank you for showing me that."

"Does that mean..." Callum slid a little closer to her.

"You, good sir, need your rest. You almost died. And from what it sounds like, your mother is terrifying. I need to return you in one piece to her."

"There's nothing like speaking of a man's mother to take the wind out of his sails," Callum complained.

Lily laughed and gently patted his cheek. "I would very much like it if you would hold my hand while we sleep." She knew if she let him hold her...well, it would be game over. This pull between them was intensifying, and now that she had this silky nightgown on, she felt like her senses were heightened.

"I wish for more. Maybe…in our dreams…you will permit me to come closer. Will you meet me in the tower room? The one you wrote about?"

"I'll try," Lily said. Truthfully, she had no idea if she could control her dreams that way, but hoped she would be able to see him there. Dream Lily was much more confident in taking what she wanted. It was where she felt more in charge of her world, and less like a scared and jumpy mouse.

"Codladh, mo grha."

Sleep, my love. Lily smiled to herself as his hand closed over hers and sleep claimed her. It was the fastest she'd fallen asleep in ages, and for once she felt safe and at ease in her life.

"You found me." Callum smiled to her from across the tower room and Lily whirled in a circle. She'd seen him moments before in her bed, and yet here they were, together, in a room of her dreams. The lines between reality and fantasy were blurring even more and Lily began to realize that she no longer cared. If this was where her happiness was to be found…then she would take it.

"You found *me*." Lily laughed.

"That I did. I would follow you to the ends of the earth, mo ghrá." Callum walked toward her, resplendent in dark leather pants and a loose white tunic. His hair was bound back by a leather cord at the nape and his eyes held all the heat the room lacked. "You do like your colorless rooms, don't you?"

"I guess I hadn't realized it." Lily laughed again as she

turned and studied the room. White marble lined the walls, a white four-poster bed held flowing white curtains, and there were even white candles scattered around the room. "This is positively virginal, isn't it?"

"Maybe you wanted the symbolism for our first time together," Callum said. He stopped, inches from her, and Lily felt the punch of his power as it vibrated against her skin.

"How would you change it?" Lily asked, tilting her chin to look up at him as heat pooled low in her body.

"You need color," Callum said instantly, and turning, he flicked a hand at the room. Lily peered around him, her mouth open, to see the once white and somewhat cold room had turned into a lush paradise. Purple silk sheets covered the bed and lush greenery was tucked in gold pots around the room. The candles had vanished, and above them hung a ceiling full of stars, hovering over them of their own accord.

"You're incredible," Lily whispered. "You see me like nobody else has. You think I'm more than I am."

"No, I think you're *you*. An amazing, strong, and fantastic woman I'm blessed to have as my fated mate. I'm not the one who undervalues you. You are. But I believe in time you'll lose that habit. I can't wait until you harness your power," Callum said, and held out a hand. Lily took it, knowing she was helpless not to, for the pull between them was too strong.

"But I can't harness my power. I'm not magick," Lily said, taking his hand and feeling a current run up her arm. She shivered as he brought her hand to his lips.

"Of course you are. Everyone is, my darling, if they believe enough."

Lily desperately wanted to trust his words. She wanted to be the fierce warrior goddess – confident in her own power – who could take on the world. Maybe, just for tonight – in this most private of spaces – she could be.

"I might need to borrow your belief for a little bit. But I'll get better." Lily reached out and did what she'd been wanting to since she'd brought Callum home. She ran her hands over his chest, relishing in the hard muscles she found there, and farther up to twine around his neck. Tilting her head up, she met his eyes. "Kiss me."

"With pleasure, mo ghrá." Callum dropped his lips to hers in a whisper of a kiss that seared its way straight to her toes. Seeming to know what she needed, he teased her mouth gently as he slowly walked her backward to the bed. Nerves wrestled with excitement in the pit of her stomach, and Lily shoved the thoughts away. She wanted this moment to be hers, unencumbered by the past, free to feel.

She pulled from the kiss as they reached the bed. Turning, Lily put her hand to Callum's chest, her heart pounding as she looked up at him.

She pushed him.

A flash of delight crossed his face as Callum fell easily back onto the silk sheets, laughing up at her, a challenge in his eyes. Lily knew what he was asking – what he needed – and she was going to be the one in charge tonight.

Climbing onto the bed, she straddled his waist, her satin nightgown pooling around him. The stars flickered overhead, coating them in a warm light, and Callum's smile flashed white in his face.

"I've been wanting to do this since I first met you. In my dreams...and now in real life," Lily said.

"I've ached for you," Callum said, his voice hoarse as he watched her. Still, he didn't touch her.

For she hadn't asked him to. What power this was – to know that someone wanted her so badly but would respect her wishes. He valued her, even when it taxed his restraint. A faint sheen of sweat had broken on his brow, and she reveled in knowing she was capable of making a fae prince break a sweat. Slowly, ever so slowly, Lily reached for the hem of her nightgown and pulled it inch by inch up her body. Callum's muscles tightened under her thighs and she could feel his hardness pressed at her back.

"You're incredible," he breathed, his eyes roaming her body. Everywhere he looked, she felt her skin heat beneath his gaze, and she wondered if it was his magick making her feel this way.

"My body feels warm...alive...when you look at me. Is that your magick? Is it a spell?" Lily asked, running her hands lightly along her thighs and up her waist.

"No," Callum gasped, "That is our magick. Fated mates. You'll feel me in many ways."

"So when you look here..." Lily cupped a breast in her palm. "I will feel your touch."

"Something like that," Callum bit out.

"It's...almost electric..." Lily gasped as her nipple responded, heat rushing over the sensitive nub.

"Lily..." Callum groaned and bucked under her. Lily

laughed and put one hand out to his chest, forcing him to stay.

"And what about when I look at you? Will you feel me?" she wondered, her eyes caressing his body. Callum closed his eyes and swore, and Lily felt his hardness jerk once more at her back.

"Incredible," she said. "I find you intensely attractive." Leaning over, she trailed her fingers over his shoulders and leaned forward to capture his lips with her mouth. She stayed there, teasing him a moment, testing to see if he would lose his control. Still, his hands stayed at his sides, the sheets in knots at his fists.

She smiled against his mouth as her breasts brushed his chest, heightening the sensation that was building low in her core. Slowly, she took her lips from his and began to kiss her way down his body. He froze as she traced her tongue down his chest, tracing a nipple, before following the ridges of his muscular stomach lower. She took her time, circling the area she wanted to tease the most, easing lower until she found where she wanted to be.

Smiling up at him, she took his length in her mouth, laughing as he swore to the stars above. "I swear, Lily, if you don't let me touch you, I may have to wake you up and show you who is in charge."

"I'm pretty sure I'm in charge." Lily pulled back and shot him a sassy grin.

"You are." Callum groaned, bringing both his hands to his face. "Always and forever, you are in charge. But you're killing me here...Lily. I'm dying to touch you. Please, let me love you, mo ghrá."

"You may," Lily said, primly.

Callum sat up so fast she almost toppled off the bed. Instead, he caught her and flipped her on her back, running his hands over her body in one delicious movement. Lily arched her back and moaned as his mouth found her breasts and lust speared through her as his hand found her heat. Tirelessly, he worked her to the edge, bringing her over in a wave of lust that hit her so hard she threw her head back on the bed and stared blindly at the stars above. When his mouth replaced his hand, Lily shrieked as he teased her most sensitive spot, bringing her rapidly to the cusp once again.

"Stop, stop, please…" Lily begged, and Callum pulled back, his eyes almost feral as he stared at her from between her legs.

"What do you need?" he panted.

"I want you. All of you. Right now," she whimpered. In an instant, Callum's pants disappeared and Lily speared up from the bed, pushing her hand against his chest to flip him over. Understanding her need, he rolled, pulling her on top of him so that she could be in charge.

"I've dreamt of you. For years now." Callum met her eyes. "I've wanted this for so long. Please promise me one thing…"

"What do you need?" Lily asked, echoing his earlier sentiment.

"Promise me you'll try to love me. Before you give up or get scared or become nervous…promise me you'll try."

"I…" Lily wanted so desperately to tell him that she already did. But she wasn't sure if she could trust herself yet. When she said those words – she had to *know* it. "I promise."

"That's all I ask, mo ghrá."

Lily shifted and took him inside her, her eyes never leaving his, and leaned over to meet his lips as together they found their own rhythm and made their own promises to each other.

When Lily awoke, the storm had gone but another one raged inside her. Turning, she met Callum's eyes and smiled, beckoning him to her with one finger.

And this time, he loved her in real life.

Chapter Eleven

"CALLUM!"

Lily squealed and pulled the covers up as a woman appeared at the foot of their bed. Well, a woman – but a very magickal one at that. Purple sparks positively shot off her as she skidded to a stop by Callum's side.

"Mother," Callum said.

Lily groaned and pulled the sheet over her face.

"You're alive." The queen's voice caught.

"I am. But I think you're embarrassing Lily. Will you wait in the front room? She has a thing about nudity."

"*I* don't have a thing. *Everyone* has a thing. It's not polite to greet people naked," Lily hissed.

"See?"

"Well, of course she does, dear. She's human. They are known for being a bit prudish in that department. I'll just be out front."

How could anyone call her a prude when she was naked in bed with a fae prince, Lily did not know.

"Hi," Callum said. He'd ducked his head under the sheet and was grinning at her. "My mum's here."

"I noticed," Lily said, dryly.

"Fancy meeting her?"

"Do I have a choice?" Lily grumbled.

"Of course you do. You always will, with me. I promised you that," Callum said, his face serious.

"Thank you," Lily said, and reached out to trail a finger across his lips. "I can't get much more embarrassed now, so I might as well meet her. Think you can magick me into some clothes?" She was only half-joking.

"Sure," Callum said, and snapped his fingers.

"Not what I had in mind." Lily glared at him as she looked down at a leather dominatrix bodysuit.

"Oh, right. Something more suitable then?"

"Maybe I shouldn't have saved you from the beach," she said.

"Ah, there's my fierce one," Callum grinned and snapped his finger again.

Lily looked down to find simple dark jeans and a deep purple top covered her body. "I'll admit, this is really convenient. You like your purple, don't you?"

"It suits you. You should wear it often."

Lily pulled back the cover and stood in front of the mirror, smiling a bit at the tenderness between her legs. Callum was an excellent lover, but she liked to think she had held her own as well. Her eyes looked bright in the mirror, and a healthy pink flush tinged her cheeks. Maybe she *would* wear purple more often, Lily thought, and went to wind her hair up in a knot.

"Leave it down. I like it," Callum said, passing her on the way to the front room.

"Sure, why not?" Lily said, and stopped herself from pulling it up. Her hair did look nice down – he was right.

"Mother," Callum said from where he stood with his arm around a stunningly beautiful woman, who had her arms wrapped around his waist. "This is Lily. She saved my life."

Lily's mouth dropped open when the woman rushed to her and gathered Lily into her arms. When she felt the woman's shoulders shake, she realized quickly that his mother was crying. Putting her arms around her back, Lily patted the woman and led her toward one of the chairs by the fire.

"I'm sorry. I'm so sorry. I'm not usually one for fits of emotion like this, but I'd heard he was dead. I was delivered false news." Callum's mother wiped her eyes with a cloth that he handed her.

"This is Queen Aurelia, also known as my mother."

"Nice to meet you," Lily said, and tried to do a bit of a curtsy. The woman was intimidating with her pink hair, gorgeous features, and light violet eyes.

"Oh, please, don't bother with pretense. I'm forever indebted to you, Lily. You've saved my son and I will not soon forget this," Queen Aurelia said.

"What news were you given?" Callum asked, gently nudging Lily into the other chair and dropping to the floor to rest his shoulder against his mother's leg. Lily understood what he was doing – the queen clearly needed reassurance he was alive.

"I was told you drowned. Nolan's boat returned empty.

The water fae swore you went under and said they couldn't save you."

"They lied."

"So I've come to understand. They were being mighty fluid in their stories, and it took great magick to get an understanding of what happened."

"Will we go to battle?"

"It might come to that." Queen Aurelia sighed. "I had hoped to avoid it. I understand their anger right now."

"They tried to kill me."

"An unforgiveable offense. Had they succeeded, we'd be at war right now and they wouldn't win."

"I think they realized that. It was part of what the storm was about the last couple of days."

"Which is why it took me so long to trace you. It was like your magick had winked out. I thought you were gone." Queen Aurelia reached down and squeezed Callum's shoulder.

Lily's heart clenched at the thought of losing him. It... well, it felt terrifying. Already their link had grown stronger, and being without him, a man she'd only known for two days, now seemed unfathomable. But *had* she known him only for two days? Lily had realized in their dreamwalk last night that she had been getting to know him for ages.

Falling in love with him in her dreams for years now.

She let out a whoosh of air, and both the fae looked at her.

"I'm sorry, I just feel so badly for you. It must have been so awful to think he was gone," Lily said to Queen Aurelia.

"It was." The queen studied her with those unnerving violet eyes. "You care for him."

"I…yes, I do."

"Is it love?"

"Mother, that is between us. The first time she says it is not going to be because some woman browbeats her into it," Callum said.

"I'm hardly browbeating. I'm merely asking a question."

"And I've asked her to promise me she would try. I love her, Mother. She is my fated mate. But she gets to decide in her own time how she feels about me."

"Hmpf. It's not like you're difficult to love. I don't see what the problem is," Queen Aurelia said.

"You can't force these things." Callum pointed out.

Lily stood up and walked away, leaving them both in the sitting room. It didn't seem like she actually needed to be there for the conversation, and she wanted a tea and a scone more than she wanted her next breath.

"Lily."

"Yes?" Lily turned from where she'd put the pot of tea on the stove.

"It's been brought to my attention that perhaps I'm being a bit pushy. You see, I want nothing more than my son's happiness, is all. Forgive me if I was rude."

"You're forgiven." Lily grinned at her. "Would you like a scone and some tea?"

"I…well, yes, that would be nice. Then I think I've been given my marching orders for now. Do say you'll come visit, won't you? I'd love to get to know you better."

"With the fae? Visit you at home?" Lily's mouth dropped open.

"Of course."

"I would love nothing more. I have a million questions to ask about the fae."

"You might enjoy a visit to our library, then. There's a lot of fae history to be found there."

"That sounds like heaven," Lily breathed, and put out a plate of scones and pulled clotted cream from the fridge.

"Lily's a writer, Mother," Callum said, coming to stand by Lily.

"Is she really? That's fantastic."

"I'm not...no, I'm not..." Lily caught Callum's look. "Okay, yes, I'm working on some stories right now. I haven't published yet."

"Well, we'll have a party when you do." Queen Aurelia accepted the cup of tea.

Despite being woken up by her lover's mother while naked in bed, Lily decided that the morning actually had turned out as one of her better mornings. The queen had turned out to be quite vivacious and funny, and Lily was looking forward to seeing her again. Wisely not over-staying her welcome, Queen Aurelia had left with hugs for them both and a promise to keep Callum updated on the situation with the water fae.

"Finally, we're alone again," Callum said once his mother had departed. Lily laughed as he hoisted her on the counter and positioned himself between her legs. She slid into his arms, loving the feeling of his lips on hers, and lost herself to his kiss.

A sharp knock sounded at the door.

"What is this? The main portal?" Callum griped. Lily could only assume that was kind of like Grand Central Station for his world.

"Who is it?" Lily asked. She slid off the counter and went to stand by the door.

"Bianca."

"Oh, hi!" Lily said, pulling the door open to see Bianca and Seamus standing at her door. Seamus froze and then dipped low in a bow while both Lily and Bianca gaped at him.

"Sir," Seamus said.

"Hello, my brethren. Please, be at ease here."

"You two know each other?" Bianca asked, looking between the two men.

"Do you women never listen? I told you at the pub the other night. Prince Callum. Fae royalty. Next in line to the throne."

"Oh, he had the right Callum, then, didn't he? Good for you, girl." Bianca winked at Lily, who could only laugh.

"Can I invite you in for tea?" Lily asked, ignoring the groan that came from behind her.

"No, thank you. We're just dropping your car off for you now that the weather's cleared. And we wanted to extend an invite for tonight."

"What's tonight?" Lily asked.

"It's Christmas Eve," Seamus said. "There's always a big party at Gallagher's Pub. We thought you'd like to come and meet some more of the people in town. Now that you're accepting magick is real, you'll fit in even better."

"I'm doing my best to understand and accept it all. It may take a bit more time," Lily admitted.

"It took me a bit, too. But, since we were in the middle of a quest at the time, I couldn't do much but put my big girl panties on and fight for the treasures." Bianca said.

"Oh!" Callum snapped his fingers. "That is why your names are so familiar. You're *the* Bianca and Seamus."

"We are." Seamus's smile stretched wide in his face.

"What does he mean?" Lily asked.

"We aided some protectors on their quest to protect the seekers who were meant to find the four treasures. It ended an ancient curse. Kind of a big thing in the fae realm." Bianca studied her nails as if it was no big deal.

"She's acting cool, but she was quite chuffed about our win for years after." Seamus poked her and Bianca giggled.

"I was! It was *so* cool to win a fae battle."

"We are in your debt." Callum bowed his head to Seamus, whose face flushed pink.

"Wow, there is a lot of in people's debt being thrown around today," Lily said.

"What happened?" Bianca asked.

"My mother walked in on us in bed. She'd thought I died and I told her Lily saved me. She was very grateful."

"Oh…oh, you poor dear. What a way to meet the mother-in-law," Bianca hissed between her lips.

Lily laughed, though her heart did a little dance at the word *mother-in-law*.

"Bianca. Stop chattering on. It's freezing out here."

"Oh, all right then. If you'd put some weight on, you wouldn't be cold so often," Bianca griped.

"But then I wouldn't have an excuse to have you warm me up."

Lily grinned as they walked to their car, promising to see them tonight. Closing the door, she squealed as Callum swept her up in his arms.

"I'm a bit cold myself. Fancy a way to warm me up?"

"I have a few ideas…"

Chapter Twelve

"I'VE NEVER BEEN to Christmas. What are the expectations?" Callum asked as they got ready to go to the pub that night.

"You…wait, you've never been to a Christmas party?"

"No, it isn't a religion we follow. I know there is a man in a red suit who gives presents. Is that Jesus?"

"Um, no." Lily laughed. "That's Santa Claus. He's sort of a children's storybook character. Once you grow up you no longer believe in Santa Claus."

"That's kind of sad. Who brings your presents then?"

"Usually your loved ones."

Callum looked distraught for a moment. "So I need a gift?"

"No, gosh, Callum, no. You don't have to give presents. You weren't expecting Christmas. You've had no time to shop."

"But it is traditional to bring gifts for friends too?"

"Yes, traditionally."

"Let me think about this for a moment." Callum

returned to the bedroom while Lily turned a circle in the main room. Spying her leather book, she grabbed it and tucked it into her purse. Maybe, just maybe, if she was feeling confident enough, she'd give Callum her book as a gift. It didn't just hold one story – it held every dream she'd ever had of him. Frankly, it was one long love note. Her stomach twisted in knots, thinking about giving this to him, but it also felt right.

"I think I'm ready now," Callum said. He came into the living room with his arms full of wrapped gifts.

"What…how…" Lily held up a hand. "Never mind. Magick."

"Correct. We should be heading out."

"I hope you didn't go over the top. No need for anything fancy," Lily said, worried now her gift would seem silly.

"I think I got the right gifts for everyone. Maybe I can be Santa Claus."

"Maybe." She laughed as they left the cottage only to draw up short at the man standing in the beam of her outdoor light.

"Lily."

"Bruce. What are you doing here?" Lily felt like someone had thrown a bucket of ice water over her head, and her thoughts scrambled in her brain. On high alert, Lily placed a hand over where her heart now raced in her chest.

Lily heard the packages drop and she put out a hand to grab Callum's arm as he attempted to pass her. A thread of fear slicked through her. "Just wait, Callum. Please."

"This is the man who hurt you?" Callum turned to Lily, his voice low.

"It is. Just...let's see what he wants."

"He gets five minutes and then I will kill him."

"No, please. I can't handle any more violence..." Lily whispered, pressing a kiss to his cheek. Holding his hand, she turned to Bruce.

He looked weak, she realized, next to her new lover. He was much shorter than Callum, not nearly as fit, and his hair was going. What had she seen in him again? In an instant, all of the anger she had for him vanished. She realized that he no longer had any power over her, only her own thoughts did.

"I see you already hooked up with some lad. I'd expect it of someone like you."

She ignored his dig. "How did you find me, Bruce?"

"The post office sent a card confirming your change of address."

Lily closed her eyes. She hadn't been as smart as she'd thought. "Why are you here?"

"You left me with no explanation. No reason. Just up and gone in the middle of the night. What kind of woman are you?" Bruce spit on the ground, and Lily felt Callum's arm go rigid. To his credit, he didn't do anything, as he'd promised her. For at least another few minutes, that is. Fear crept through Lily as she thought of what could happen.

"The kind that won't stand up to abuse."

"Please, it wasn't...god, you *always* do this. You make something big out of nothing. Listen, I'm sorry about that. I had too much to drink. I wasn't thinking. You can't leave over something like that. You know I'd never hurt you. I love you."

"You did hurt me. And you've hurt me for years with your words and your actions. I had every right to leave you. Please just leave me alone."

"So that's it? You're going to throw it all away to shack up with this guy? We had a life together. We had *everything* together. What are people going to say? Everyone's asking about you and I keep saying you're sick."

"You're lying to people about me? That's ridiculous, Bruce. For once in your life, be honest. Even if you can't with anyone else – be honest with yourself. You are abusive. You need help."

"That's a damn lie. I won't have you sullying my name." A flash of rage crossed over Bruce's face, and he stepped forward.

And so did Callum.

"Wait, please, he's weak," Lily protested.

Callum turned and met her eyes. "Do you trust me?"

"I do."

Turning, he strode forward, so fast that Bruce didn't have time to react. He held his palm to Bruce's head and Bruce froze in place, not moving a muscle. Lily's heart twisted as a glow shimmered around him, and then Callum stepped back until he was by her side once more. Wrapping an arm around her shoulders, he waited quietly.

Bruce blinked at them both and then whirled around in a full circle before looking back at them.

"Are you all right, mate?" Callum asked.

"I'm not sure. I think I'm lost. Excuse me, miss, can you tell me where I am?"

"Miss?" Lily blinked at Bruce.

"You're in Grace's Cove, mate. West coast of Ireland."

"Well, that's silly. I live by Dublin."

"Long drive home for you tonight. Might want to get a room at a hotel."

"Huh. This is just the weirdest thing. Did I have a night out with my mates? Is that how I ended up here?"

"Must be. Safe home for you, then," Callum said as Bruce walked to his car. Turning, he looked around again and shrugged once before getting in his car and driving off.

"Did you…did you erase his memory?" Lily asked.

"I erased all memories he had of you. Including your presence in his life. I also tampered with the bit in him that makes him abusive. He'll be docile as a lamb for his next girlfriend now. You can let him go."

"I…oh." Tears blinked into Lily's eyes. The fear of running into Bruce again had been a weight she'd planned to always carry on her shoulders. But now, it was gone… just like that. "Oh, maybe you *are* Santa Claus!"

Lily threw her arms around Callum's neck and kissed him thoroughly. His hands came to her waist and he lifted her to spin her under the cold star-filled night.

"I told you I would protect you. Since you wouldn't let me use violence, I had to get creative."

"This is even better. I don't like meeting violence with violence. Thank you," She kissed him again. "I feel truly free now."

"And I need a pint, pretty lady. Care to be my date to my first Christmas party?"

"I'd love nothing more," Lily said.

Chapter Thirteen

THE PARTY WAS ALREADY in full swing when they arrived – Lily could hear it all the way down the street.

"It sounds like they've got a band. Can you dance?" Callum asked, carrying the load of presents next to her.

"I've been known to a time or two." She laughed and then stopped under the mistletoe hanging at the door.

"What's wrong?"

"Mistletoe." Lily smiled at his confused look. "You are supposed to kiss the person you get caught under the mistletoe with."

"I like these traditions," Callum said. Leaning over his pile of gifts, he kissed her softly under the mistletoe. "I love you."

"I…" Lily said, and the door swung open from the pub.

"Got another one!" an old man crowed from where he perched on a stool by the door.

"Mr. Murphy?" Callum asked.

"That's me!"

"I've a gift for you," Callum said, and nodded to a red package on top.

"That's grand. I love gifts." Mr. Murphy beamed and ripped the paper open with the same reckless abandon of a child. "A new cap! That's great. Mine has worn a bit and my head's been cold." Mr. Murphy pulled off his faded brown newsboy cap and tucked his new gray tartan cap on his head.

"It suits you," Lily said, smiling at him.

"Lucky girl to catch a lad like that," Mr. Murphy said.

"I'm lucky to have her."

"Aye, that's the truth of it. Women are the best gifts in the world."

"Callum! Lily!" Bianca called from a booth across the room, and they made their way through the dancing crowd to where Callum could drop his packages on the table.

"Have you been shopping then?" Bianca laughed at Callum.

"It's my first Christmas! I wanted to be prepared. Oh, here, this one's for you," he said, pulling a package from the pile as Cait appeared at his side.

"Now that's a fancy trick, isn't it, seeing as we haven't properly met." Cait eyed Callum and the package he held out to her. "You've already wowed Mr. Murphy. He thinks you're Santa Claus."

"I hope it suits you," Callum said, winking at Cait.

"Cait, this is…Callum," Lily stumbled, not sure if she should introduce him as her boyfriend or not.

"He's fae royalty, Cait." Seamus said.

"You're welcome here," Cait said, and Lily grinned when she didn't bow. Instead she shot Callum a measuring look before opening her package. "Well, now. Isn't that lovely?"

She held up a crystal ornament in the shape of an elephant, the facets of crystal catching the light above and sending rainbows across the table.

"It's perfect for you, Cait." Bianca said.

"I just went to see the elephants in Africa. It was a trip of a lifetime at that. I'll fill you in when I'm not packed to my elbows in pints. Thank you, for this kind gift." Cait reached up and smacked a kiss on Callum's cheek before darting away.

"She'll be back with a pint soon enough." Bianca promised.

"And who do we have here?" A woman, with tumbling curls and piled in colorful jewelry, arrived at their table.

"Aislinn, this is Lily and Callum. Lily is new to town."

"You're fae," Aislinn said, sizing up Callum.

He blinked down at her and then laughed. "Aye, you've the right of it then."

"How did she know that?" Lily demanded.

"I told you there's powerful magick here. She's one of Grace O'Malley's descendants." Bianca nodded. "Also a famous artist. She can see auras and all sorts of fun stuff."

"For you," Callum said. He rummaged in the pile and handed her a box.

"A gift? For me? Isn't that interesting?" Aislinn mused, leaning against the booth. A tumble of bracelets jingled at her wrist as she opened her package. "Is this a travel easel?"

"Yes, but also for when you're recuperating."

"This is a smart gift." Aislinn studied Callum. "I like you."

"Thank you," Callum said.

"Recuperating from what?" Bianca demanded.

"I haven't told anyone." Aislinn grimaced. "But I have to have knee surgery."

"What? Why are you standing up then?" Bianca jumped up.

"Because it hurts to sit too long. Kira will be coming back to watch the store for me."

"Kira is Aislinn's daughter," Bianca said to Lily.

"Why are you standing?" A man loomed over Aislinn.

"Baird, I just needed a moment. The knee hurts when I bend it."

"I have a spot for you where you can put your leg up. Over there. Now either you sit and put your leg up as promised, or I am taking you home."

"But...fine," Aislinn grumbled. "This is Callum. He brought me a gift. Maybe I'll take him home instead of you if you keep bullying me."

Baird laughed and wrapped his arm around his wife's waist. "I'd like to see him try. I may be older, but love's on my side."

"He's the right of it...love wins." Callum slid Lily a look.

"Awww," Bianca said, fanning her face. "I'm so happy for you both. You looked positively shell-shocked when you were here the other day."

"It's been a very enlightening couple of days. Do you know a woman named Fiona?"

"Fiona visited you?" Cait asked, coming to their table with drinks. "Tell me everything."

"But…it's kind of a long story."

"I've got help at the bar. If it's Fiona, it's important."

Lily relayed the story as quickly as she could. "You know her?"

"Aye, we know and love her. She's Keelin's gran. Keelin and Gracie aren't here tonight, but you'll meet them soon. They live not far from your cottage. Gracie is magickal as all get out, so you'll get on great. But Fiona, she was a wild woman for the books. Her knowledge of healing and magicks was legendary."

"Thank you," Fiona said from over Cait's shoulder.

Lily gasped and held a hand to her mouth.

"How many times have I warned you about sneaking up on me?" Cait shot Fiona a look.

"It's hardly sneaking. You knew I was here."

"I can see you. Like right now. In front of me," Lily broke in. "Is that…how can I do that? I thought the other night was because it was an emergency."

"Fiona shows herself to those she considers family. Welcome," Cait said. With that, she disappeared to get a handle on the crowd packed around the bar.

"I have a gift for you as well," Callum said, smiling at Fiona, "and I must extend to you my eternal thanks. The fae are indebted to you. My mother has made it known that should you ever need something, do not hesitate to call upon us."

"I appreciate that. One never knows what the future will bring." Fiona's mouth dropped open as a fuzzy puppy appeared in her arms. "You got me a puppy? I didn't know I could have a puppy!"

"You can, it appears." Callum grinned as tears filled Fiona's eyes.

"You're killing me here," Lily said, her own eyes shining with tears. "I had no idea I could see ghosts. And now I know spirit puppies are a thing."

"I have to go show John. I'll stop by later," Fiona crowed, and winked out of sight.

"That might have been the sweetest thing I've ever seen." Bianca sighed and leaned against Seamus.

"She's quite content in the afterlife but has missed having a puppy. It was a simple thing to arrange for saving my life."

"I'm beginning to realize I have a lot to learn about your magick," Lily said.

"Take all the time you need." Callum leaned into her. "Preferably between the sheets."

"Where's my gift?" Bianca demanded, and Seamus covered his face with his hand.

"I'm sorry, sir."

"No, she's absolutely right. It's rude of me to give out gifts in front of her, but not for her. Here is yours."

"I'm excited. I love prezzies!" Bianca crowed, bouncing in her seat as she unwrapped the book. "Oh...oh, would you look at that? It's – why, is this an antique? I've never seen this book before."

"It's not of the human world. It's a historical accounting of fae history from our personal library."

Bianca looked positively gobsmacked. For the first time since Lily had met her, the woman had nothing to say.

"I think you broke her," Seamus observed. "Say 'thank you, Prince Callum.'"

"Just Callum," Callum broke in quickly, looking around.

"I could hug you! This is the best gift I've ever gotten aside from my Seamus here. Oh, I want to go home and read this right now. Can you imagine how much I can corroborate between our history and theirs? This will take months to cross-reference!" Bianca's face lit with joy.

"Well, that's her out of me hair for the next several months," Seamus joked.

"And for you, Seamus, in thanks for your service." Callum handed him a slim package wrapped in silver. Seamus carefully peeled back the paper to reveal a small wooden box. Opening it, he took out an intricately carved knife.

"It's…one of the royal knives," Seamus whispered.

"With our blessing," Callum bowed his head to him.

"I'm sure you'll be telling me all about what that does, but for now you'd better tuck that away before someone thinks we're getting violent," Bianca whispered.

"Oh, I like this song," Lily said, humming the first haunting bars. "Why do I know this?"

"Because it's our song," Callum said. He pulled her up from the booth and tugged her through the crowd to the dance floor. Christmas lights draped across the ceiling, along the walls, and garlands wrapped the booths. A fire danced in the little fireplace, and the band in the front booth played their song as Callum swept her into his arms.

"Larraim ort mo ghrá…"

"I don't think I've ever had so much fun at a Christmas party before," Lily laughed in the car on the way home. "Callum, you were incredible. I think people think you might be the real Santa Claus."

"It's quite fun, this gift-giving tradition of yours. I like seeing people smile. Fae are addicted to joy, you know."

"Are they really?"

"Well, maybe not addicted, but we are a joyous bunch. Tonight was grand fun."

"Wait…where are we? I wasn't paying attention." Lily peered into the dark when Callum cut the engine.

"Walk with me, my pretty lady, on a cold winter's night?"

"Why not?" She accepted his arm as he helped her from the car. Only when she stood up did she realize where they were. "You brought me to the cove."

"I did. I needed to see it again. With you."

"Oh, Callum, it was a terrible night there. Are you certain you want to relive it?"

"Aye, it's important to face your fears."

Lily looped her arm through his, her heart pounding as they made their way to the edge of the cove. Though the wind had picked up, it was nothing like the storm of the days before, and even the soft light of the moon was enough to see their path to the edge of the cliff walls. Once there, they paused and looked over the edge in silence.

A brilliant blue light split the depths of the water, bouncing its reflection across the cliff walls.

"It's a far way down," Callum said. Turning, he put his

arms around Lily, pulling her into his warmth. "And you carried me. All the way up and home."

"Not without help."

"You still did it. Do you know what that light means?"

"I think so. Yes."

"Do you want to tell me?"

"You don't know?" Lily tilted her head up to look at him.

"I have an idea, but no, I don't know all the magick in the world."

"First, I have a gift for you," Lily stepped back.

"Aye, and I have one for you."

"Do you? Let me see," she demanded, poking at him until he laughed. Reaching into his pocket, he pulled out a small velvet bag. He handed it to Lily.

"Oh, it's hard to see, let me…" She glanced up as a gold star came and hovered over her head, providing light to see by. "Right. A star. As one does."

"What was your solution going to be?"

"I was going to use my iPhone flashlight. But this is much fancier."

"We do like our fancy bits," Callum laughed.

"Oh, Callum, this is exquisite," Lily said. She held the necklace to the light so that the amethyst shone brightly. "I've never seen such a beautiful piece."

"It's from the royal vault. You'll be able to travel freely between worlds with me if you so choose. And it comes with the blessing of my parents."

Lily's heart skipped and she turned to him, her smile tremulous. "Will you put it on me? I'm scared to drop it."

"Of course." Callum's hands were warm at her neck,

and she shivered at his touch, feeling tendrils of lust work through her.

"How does it look?" Lily preened for him.

"Like it's home."

"Oh…" Lily held a hand to her heart. "My gift isn't so fancy, but I don't…well, it's just…"

"Hand it over woman." Callum put his hand out.

"Right, okay. This is, well…here." Lily pulled the book out of her bag and handed it to him.

"You're giving me your book?" Callum asked. "Have you finished your story?"

"Actually, several of them. See, I've written down every dream I've ever had of you. It's our story, really. It's my love letter…to you. To us, really. I just thought you might like to see it. Or have it. I don't know," Lily fumbled, and then her lips were caught by his. For a moment, they stood there, their hearts hung in tender balance.

"I love you, Callum," she whispered against his lips. "I've been loving you for years now. I just didn't know you could be real."

"My sweet Lily. My fated mate. I'm so lucky to have found you. Thank you for the gift of your love. I'll treasure it always."

"It's what the light means." Lily pulled back and rested her cheek against his chest, turning to look at the shining blue water far below. "Bianca told me that Grace O'Malley, though wild and fierce, was also a believer in true love. The cove shines in the presence of true love."

"Fated mates, we are."

"For a lifetime and more…"

Have you fallen in love with Prince Callum and Lily's story? If so, I'm delighted to share that you can continue to read about the Royal Court of the Fae, along with fan favorites, Bianca & Seamus, in my upcoming series: The Wildsong Series. Read on for a sneak-peak of chapter 1.

Don't forget - the Mystic Cove series continues on with Wild Irish Sage. Enjoy!

Pre-order Song of the Fae today and get ready for an enthralling return to Ireland's magical shores.

Song of the Fae
Book 1 in the Wildsong Series.

Chapter 1

THE DOOR to Gallagher's Pub slammed open with such force that the musicians tucked in the front booth fell silent and the crowd gaped as a man strode in from the storm that raged outside.

The Prince of Fae had arrived.

Judging from the furious wave of energy that crackled around him, as though he controlled the very storm itself, Prince Callum was ready for battle.

"Oh shite," Bianca breathed from where she sat, tucked in a booth next to her husband Seamus, along with Callum's right-hand man, Nolan. In seconds, Seamus muttered a complicated spell and threw a magickal bubble across the room, concealing Callum from the view of the crowd. For a moment, everyone looked around in confusion, and then a woman jumped up and ran to close the door. From outside the spell, it would look as though the group at the table continued to enjoy an easy-going conversation.

"Just the storm blowing the door open." Cait, owner of

Gallagher's Pub, shot Callum a look from where she manned the bar and the music commenced.

Thunder roared overhead, shaking the windows of the pub, and Cait ducked under the passthrough and went head-to-head with the Prince. Though she wasn't Fae, Cait had a magickal bloodline that fueled her confidence.

"That's enough of that now. You'll be replacing any windows you break." Cait's voice was low. Callum brushed her aside like she was a gnat and Bianca's swift hiss of breath was enough to assure Nolan that very few people were ballsy enough to treat Cait that way. Not to mention the fact that it was rare for Callum to be out-right rude.

Which meant something was very, very wrong.

He'd never seen the Prince like this before. In all the years he had stood by his side, both in battle and in over-seeing the royal court of the Fae, Prince Callum lead with a cool head. Except when it came to his fated mate and one true love…Lily. The hair on the back of Nolan's neck lifted, as though darkness slithered over him, and his eyes held Callum's as the prince skidded to a stop at their table.

"Prince." Seamus bowed his head.

"Lily's missing." Callum's words fell like an icicle shattering to the ground.

Nolan was the first to speak.

"What happened? I can leave immediately. What should we do?"

Cait surprised Nolan by appearing at Callum's side once more, and she did something that no Fae would ever dare to do – she tugged Callum's hand until he was sitting on a chair in front of the table and handed him a whiskey.

"Tell us," Cait insisted.

Bianca's eyes darted to Nolan's, the pretty blonde having picked up on the break in Royal protocol, and he made a mental note that she might be useful for whatever lay before them. Because if something bad *had* happened – here in Grace's Cove and not in the Fae realm – well, they would need help navigating this world. Both Bianca and her husband, Seamus, had successfully supported the Seekers on their quest to save the Four Treasures from the Domnua, the evil fae, over two decades ago. It looked like they were about to be recruited for another quest.

Pulling his eyes back to the Prince, Nolan waited until Callum had swallowed the whiskey and then schooled his breathing. Outside their magickal bubble, the band played on and a few people had pushed chairs aside to throw themselves into a measure of complicated dance steps. Any other night, and Nolan would have joined them. When he was on duty – Nolan allowed nothing to distract him from the job. But, like all Fae, Nolan loved celebrations and where there was music, there'd often be Fae dancing just outside the awareness of humans.

"It's the Water Fae." Once more Callum leveled a fierce look at Nolan, and his insides twisted. The Water Fae were the faction of elemental Fae that Nolan commanded. It was his duty to oversee and manage their concerns and needs – which meant something, likely the Domnua, had forced the Water Fae to act out.

"You're certain?" Nolan asked, his words sharp.

"Aye, sure and I'm certain. Didn't they already try to kill me?"

It had come as a great surprise to everyone in the Fae

realm, particularly those in the Royal court, when the Water Fae had launched a surprise attack on Prince Callum, nearly drowning him on his mission to find his fated mate. Luckily, Callum had survived and had mated with his beautiful Lily, and Nolan had been left to clean up the mess with the Water Fae.

Which, he'd *thought* he'd handled…

"Sir, I met with the leader just this week."

"And what was the resolution of this meeting?"

"I met with the Water Fae on their turf – in their protected cave deep in the sea. I was quite confident that we'd left the meeting with a mutual respect and understanding. They'd brought up some concerns for me to address, and I've already made good on one of them."

"Which one?" Callum asked, his fingers clenched tightly on the whiskey glass. The rest of the table remained silent, their eyes bouncing between Callum and Nolan like they were watching a tennis match.

"They desired that the path of the human's cargo ships be amended slightly as it crossed too closely to their nurseries in the kelp. I adjusted the currents of the ocean to force the boats to give a wider berth to that particular area." Nolan had been proud of this particular feat, as it had taken careful management of many natural elements, not to mention adjusting human behavior without them being aware of it. He'd also been pleased to be able to help the Water Fae quickly, so they would understand that he was working on behalf of them as a representative in the higher realms of Fae Court.

"And that's all? Nothing else…untoward happened in this meeting?"

Nolan was shocked by the note of suspicion in Callum's voice. Not only had Nolan proven his allegiance to the prince numerous times over, but they were also friends. The accusing look in his eyes sent a shiver across the back of Nolan's neck. While Callum was known for being fair, he could also be ruthless. If there was any reason for Callum to suspect that Nolan was involved in Lily's disappearance – he'd be dead before the end of the night.

"No, sir. It was one of our better meetings. Frankly, I'm surprised by this. I was quite pleased with the results of our negotiations, and it had sounded like the elders were as well. Please, can you tell me what happened?" Nolan took a careful sip of his whiskey, the liquid burning a hot trail to his stomach.

"I only left her for a moment." Callum's voice was ragged, his eyes haunted. "I'd promised her I was going to try to light a fire like humans do." Callum waved his hand in the air. "You know, with the wood, and the flame, and the tinder…all that nonsense. She wanted to see if I would have the patience to try it without my magick, you see. It was a game, really. We were having fun…laughing. I went outside into the storm to get the firewood from the shed. She'd…she'd been standing in the doorway, just a touch in the rain, laughing out at me because she wanted to watch me do manual labor."

Bianca looked as though she wanted to make a comment about if building a fire was really manual labor but shut her mouth when Seamus touched her arm briefly. The two worked beautifully together, and were so in tune that Nolan was surprised that Seamus had even had to physically correct her.

"When I came back…wood in my arms…she was gone." Callum slammed his fist down on the table and a flash of lightning lit the sky outside the pub. In seconds, thunder followed, shaking the room with its wrath. "The door was wide open. And…just this."

Callum pulled out a piece of parchment paper and put it on the table. Nolan leaned over, not touching it for Fae magick was tricky on an easy day – and read the words.

We trade a love for a love. You've stolen our power. Now we steal your heart.

Below the words was a sketch of a talisman etched with an intricate Celtic knot. It was a drawing of the Water Fae's amulet, which was unimaginably powerful in the wrong hands, and only worn by the leader of the Water Fae. Each faction of the elemental Fae had a ruling talisman such as the amulet, and the leader always had it on hand lest it be stolen and used for wrongdoing. Panic slipped through Nolan as he met Callum's eyes.

"The amulet. It's missing."

"Aye, and they think *we* stole it."

Song of the Fae

Author's Note

I know this book comes as a surprise for many of you as I hadn't mentioned writing a Christmas story to anyone. I was craving a warm, fuzzy, story of the heart – and this is what came out when I sat down to write it. I always miss a few of my favorite characters when series are over, so was delighted to bring Bianca and Seamus back for a quick hello. To stay in my inner circle and be the first to hear about more surprises you can join my mailing list here: http://eepurl.com/1LAiz.

2020 has been a particularly tough year for everyone, and the impact of this year will likely sit deep in our souls for years to come. My hope was to provide a moment of joy and love, and perhaps even a glimmer of hope for brighter days ahead.

Happy Holidays to you all! Thanks for being the amazing and supportive readers you are. Sending light and love to you and yours.

Until I next see you, safe home will you go.

Slainté,
Tricia O'Malley

The Mystic Cove Series

Wild Irish Heart

Wild Irish Eyes

Wild Irish Soul

Wild Irish Rebel

Wild Irish Roots: Margaret & Sean

Wild Irish Witch

Wild Irish Grace

Wild Irish Dreamer

Wild Irish Christmas (Novella)

Wild Irish Sage

Wild Irish Renegade

Wild Irish Moon

"I have read thousands of books and a fair percentage have been romances. Until I read Wild Irish Heart, I never had a book actually make me believe in love."- Amazon Review

Available in audio, e-book & paperback!

The Isle of Destiny Series

ALSO BY TRICIA O'MALLEY

Stone Song

Sword Song

Spear Song

Sphere Song

Available in audio, e-book & paperback!

"Love this series. I will read this multiple times. Keeps you on the edge of your seat. It has action, excitement and romance all in one series."- Amazon Review

The Althea Rose Series

ALSO BY TRICIA O'MALLEY

Available in audio, e-book & paperback!

Available from Amazon

"Not my usual genre but couldn't resist the Florida Keys setting. I was hooked from the first page. A fun read with just the right amount of crazy! Will definitely follow this series."- Amazon Review

Also by Tricia O'Malley

STAND ALONE NOVELS

Ms. Bitch

"Ms. Bitch is sunshine in a book! An uplifting story of fighting your way through heartbreak and making your own version of happily-ever-after."

~Ann Charles, USA Today Bestselling Author

One Way Ticket

A funny and captivating beach read where booking a one-way ticket to paradise means starting over, letting go, and taking a chance on love…one more time

10 out of 10 - The BookLife Prize semi finalist

Firebird Award Winner

Pencraft Book of the year 2021

Author's Acknowledgement

A very deep and heartfelt *thank you* goes to those in my life who have continued to support me on this wonderful journey of being an author. At times, this job can be very stressful, however, I'm grateful to have the sounding board of my friends who help me through the trickier moments of self-doubt. An extra-special thanks goes to The Scotsman, who is my number one supporter and always manages to make me smile.

Please know that every book I write is a part of me, and I hope you feel the love that I put into my stories. Without my readers, my work means nothing, and I am grateful that you all are willing to share your valuable time with the worlds I create. I hope each book brings a smile to your face and for just a moment it gives you a much-needed escape.

Slainté,
Tricia O'Malley

As always, you can reach me at
info@triciaomalley.com
or feel free to visit my website at
www.triciaomalley.com.

Made in the USA
Las Vegas, NV
17 July 2022

51758751R00081